A VERY PROPER DEATH

A VERY PROPER DEATH

ALEX JUNIPER

Random House
Toronto

Published in Canada in 1990 by Random House of Canada Limited, Toronto.

∞   This book is printed on acid-free paper.

Canadian Cataloguing in Publication Data

Juniper, Alex
    A very proper death

ISBN 0-394-22137-0

I. Title.

PS8569.U656V47 1990   C813′.54   C90-094382-3
PR9199.3.J865V47 1990

Jacket Design: Brant Cowie/ArtPlus Limited
Jacket Illustration: Ken Suzana

Printed and bound in Canada

Contents

Three gamblers sit under a tree
Playing dice with the hooded man.
The hooded man has bundles three.
Winner takes all, says he.

The first player throws and wins his prize:
A very proper death.
The second wins poison; the second dies.
The third has greed in his eyes.

The third player laughs. I win, cries he.
The third player draws his knife.
The mask of the hooded man falls free.
Winner takes death, says he.

1: Death Calling

On Mt. Vernon Street, the most proper street in Boston, the automatic timer had turned the streetlights down to their post–midnight wattage. Snow collected in the cast-iron filigree (Beacon Hill long ago simply added wiring to its old gas lamps), and the dimmed electric light came through the snow and the iron scrolls in a haze, not unlike the gas glow of yesteryear. At the corner of Mt. Vernon and Charles streets, a man, half frozen, stumbled through the snow looking for a sheltered doorway or a subway grating. Somewhere a dog barked.

Halfway up the steep street, opposite Louisburg Square, Marni Verstak woke with a jolt and fumbled for the phone in the dark. God, what time was it?

"Hello?" she mumbled, her tongue clumsy with sleep.

"Could I speak to Matthew please?" It was a man's voice, quite brisk and businesslike.

"Sorry," Marni groaned. "Wrong number."

Wouldn't you know it? She hung up and squinted at her digital clock. It was 2:05, with a 9:00 a.m. business meeting looming, then her date with City Hall. She would be taking two of the most influential councillors on a tour. Not your average Boston tour, however. Not exactly the Freedom Trail, and definitely not for tourists. Gentlemen, she'd say. I'd like you to see something a little unusual in your own backyard.

A mere subway ride from City Hall, out along the Orange Line, Dudley Station, Jamaica Plain, she would wait until they were mournfully shaking their heads, sighing political sighs, and pull out her trump card. It was going to be a touch-and-go day. Demanding.

1

Which was why she had gone to bed early. Naturally, this would be
the very night some nerd would dial a wrong number at two in the
morning. Great. Just great. You would think people who made phone
calls after midnight would take more care with—

God!

The phone rang again, shrill as a scream, and Marni, in the
act of reaching for the bedside lamp, almost knocked it off
the nightstand.

"Yes?" she gasped, barely saving the lamp.

"Could I speak to Matthew please?"

"Shit," she muttered under her breath. And then, more tartly: "He
still isn't here. He never has been here. Could you please check your
number before you dial again? In case you hadn't noticed, it's the
middle of the night."

She replaced the receiver with slightly more force than usual, swore
again, softly but decisively, and snuggled back under the covers. She
closed her eyes and visualized the city councillors gaping at the house
that nestled into the seedy shadows of Jamaica Plain.

Ring, ring!

Jesus! A joker, a pervert, a loony. Someone who got his kicks from
turning women into nervous wrecks on dark nights. She groped for the
jack to disconnect the phone at the wall, but the urge to vent her
irritation and have the last word overcame her.

"Okay," she said into the receiver calmly, with a hint of boredom
*(don't sound angry or nervous, that's exactly what they're after, that's
what turns them on)*, "I've switched on my answering machine, so
you're on tape. You still have the wrong number and Matthew still isn't
here, but please feel free to talk. I'll make a police report and give them
the tape in the morning."

That should do the trick.

"Look," the voice said. "I know you must think I'm some sort of
crazy, and I'm dreadfully sorry to keep bothering you like this." The
voice was educated, formal, a gentleman's voice. It sounded vaguely
British, and there was something about the *s* sounds, there was a faint
almost-lisp, as though the tongue were a little sluggish. Or as though
the front teeth protruded a little, maybe. "The thing is, I've got to relay

an urgent message about a death in the family, and I'm sure I *do* have the right number. I've got it written down. Isn't this 555-9761?"

"Yes," Marni said contritely. "I'm sorry I was rude. That's my number, but I'm afraid there's no Matthew here and never has been."

"That's funny," the man said. "I was led to believe you were Matthew's mother."

Something that felt like a thousand volts hit Marni in the stomach and travelled to the tips of her fingers and toes like rockets. Her breath stuck in her throat.

"That's what the call is about," the man said pleasantly. "You're Marni Verstak, right? I can see you, as a matter of fact. Metaphorically speaking. I can see you in your nightgown with the quilt thrown aside, and the blue floral pattern on your sheets."

The blue floral pattern on Marni's sheets became so sharp and clear that the edges of the forget-me-nots hurt her eyes; then the pattern turned blurry, out of focus, and she had to blink, her eyes were watering so badly.

"You are single," the voice went on pleasantly, "though formerly married. Bit of a disaster, that marriage, wasn't it? You are twenty-eight years old, and you work in real estate. Young, successful, beautiful—at least in the opinion of many people, though personally I have rather different tastes. You are also Matthew's mother, and this call is about Matthew's death."

Then he hung up.

Marni felt as though she were suspended under water; she was turning blue, she could not breathe. This is a nightmare, she thought. Then she seemed to surface, and sirens were going off inside her head. Adrenaline zipped about in all directions. Her body hummed like a high-tension wire. For a moment, she pressed the receiver hard between her breasts as though it might be possible to muffle its message, to extinguish it, to make it unsay itself. She was gasping, breathing noisily like an asthmatic child, hoping against hope to wake up out of the dream.

The red numerals on her digital alarm clock blinked at her: 2:11.

Dreams don't keep time, she thought. The first call came at 2:05. I'm awake! A man *did* call. He said . . .

God! she thought. Oh God. Please please *please* let it be a crazy coincidence.

She switched on the lamp, pressed the phone buttons to get a dial tone, and began to dial the village of Wilderness in Vermont. Her fingers were shaking so badly that it took three attempts.

At last. The ringing. She imagined how the sound was shattering the deep stillness of Wilderness, a village too small even to appear in the *Texaco Touring Atlas*, just six farms and a cluster of barns and horses. *Oh please, Eva, answer!*

An answer of sorts: a sleepy voice mumbling "Wha..?", and then the crash of something knocked over in the dark.

"Eva?" Marni could hardly speak. (Was she whispering or shouting? She had no idea. The thump of her blood was deafening in her own ears.)

"Who *is* this?"

"Eva, it's me. Marni. Listen, this is urgent, I have to—"

"Marni! What the hell? What *time* is it?"

"Eva, *listen* to me. Is Matthew all right?"

"What? Of course he's all right. He's asleep in his room. What the hell are you—"

"Eva, will you go and look? Please? *Please*. This is urgent, it's a matter of life and death."

"Okay. Okay, I'm going." Marni could tell that Eva was wide awake now, that the panic had leaped from voice to voice. There was a wait, an interminable wait, there was the sound of a bass drum thumping under Marni's bones, the room was breathing in and out like an oxygen tent.

"Marni?"

Yes, she tried to whisper, though no sound came out. (Please please *please*, God!)

"He's in his bed, sleeping like a lamb. No fever, nothing wrong with his breathing. Marni, what on earth is the matter?"

"Oh, thank God." Marni was half laughing, half sobbing.

"For heaven's sake, Marni, what's going on?"

"Oh Eva, I don't know. The weirdest thing, the most terrifying thing. . . . I had this phone call, well, three calls actually, and —" There was a sound at Marni's fourth-floor window, the one against the fire-escape landing, and Marni froze. Paranoia gripped her. Suppose someone was watching her? Suppose someone could see her blue floral sheets? Suppose someone was watching Matthew? Suppose her phone was being tapped?

"Marni? Marni, answer me. What's happening? Marni?"

"Eva," she whispered. "I can't explain now. Can you just, please, take extra-special precautions?"

"Are we talking about kidnap, or what? Do you mean the Dragon Lady has found out?"

Yes, Marni thought, staring at the moving blind. It had to be. Abigail Thorpe, her mother-in-law during four years of non-marriage. A matriarch who'd stop at nothing, Andy used to say.

"Marni?"

"Yes, I'm here. I think there's someone. . . . Just take enormous care, Eva, *please*. I'll call tomorrow."

She hung up and stared at the microblinds that screened the window. The thin slats sighed and swayed, but it was the convection current from the radiators—*of course it was!*—that caused this. Marni bit her lip and stared at the blind. She was afraid to get out of bed and open it. She was afraid not to. She bit her lip and counted to ten.

When she slid from the bed, the sheets made a noise like a waterfall, the mattress shrieked, each blue flower on the pillow cases cried: *Beware.* Every step across the carpet seemed thunderous. Marni gave the dangling acrylic dowel a quarter turn and the slats of the blind winked open a crack, like sleepy eyes.

There was nothing on the fire escape landing. The bare branch of an oak scratched against the window. So that's all it was, a tree moving in the wind.

I'm going crazy, Marni thought.

She closed the blind, got back into bed, switched the lamp off, unplugged the phone, and lay awake for the rest of the night. The overly red lipsticked lips of Abigail Thorpe seemed to be everywhere, leering at her like the grin of the Cheshire Cat.

She wished she had Ainsley's home phone number, but Dr. Ainsley Wilson, for obvious reasons, could only be reached during office hours.

When dawn came, Marni reached for the pad and pencil she kept on the night table and scribbled at the top of a page: *People who know.* She underlined this. Then she wrote: 1) Eva.

But obviously Eva, who was practically a sister, a sort of twin, a kind of extension of Marni herself, obviously Eva had nothing to do with the phone call. Any more than Eva's husband, Steve, could have anything . . .

For the first time, a tiny splinter of doubt about Steve, a *very* tiny splinter, troubled Marni.

So she wrote: 2) Steve.

Who else knew about Matthew? Well, technically, the midwife who delivered him in the farmhouse bedroom in Wilderness, and the clerk with whom she registered his birth in Vermont. But all that was five years ago. True, she'd registered him as Matthew Verstak, linking him to her own family history, not his father's, but she'd given a false address, a false out-of-state address. There was no way she could be traced, was there? Besides, she couldn't even remember the midwife's name herself. She'd have to ask Eva, who'd used the same midwife three times. Salt of the earth, Eva and Steve said about the midwife. Eva and Steve had a do-it-yourself organic fervor about life.

Nevertheless, she wrote down: 3) midwife; and 4) registry office clerk.

Anyone else? She wrote down 5) and chewed her pencil. Well, there was almost Michael Lavan, until a few months ago her lover. She had planned to tell Michael, but hadn't quite, and then. . . . All this was too painful even to think about, and she blotted it out. She *hadn't* told Michael, so that was that. She could think of no one else who could possibly know, unless she counted Ainsley, which she obviously wouldn't.

So where did that leave her? She looked at her list and crossed Eva off it. She bit her lips and thought hard, then crossed off Steve's name too; but from his crossed-out name, she splayed out arrows and labeled them: *other people in Wilderness: friends and drifter contacts of Steve (druggies, old hippies, etc.).*

Yes, she thought. This was overwhelmingly the most likely source of the call. Some sickie, an old friend of Steve's, a sixties leftover who was sponging off Steve and Eva, camping out in their maple woods, had put two and two together, was after a little blackmail money for drugs.

Just that.

Marni felt immensely relieved.

It was not a serious threat, she told herself, and believed this for about two minutes. Then the blue bunches of forget-me-nots on her sheets ballooned into her vision. How could she have forgotten? It was someone (a tradesman? the plumber? someone from the condominium association? or from her own real-estate company?) who had been in the apartment; someone, therefore, who could get in again for the most legitimate, the most seemingly innocent of reasons.

The idea was chilling. She thought back. There was an electrician who checked on the dishwasher last week; there was the building super; there was a man from the television cable company; there was. . . . The list could be endless. How far back would she have to go? A week? A month?

It *has* to be one of Steve's hangers-on, said the logical part of her mind. Someone who got a job as an electrician or plumber or trash collector in my building, with a view to blackmail. So why do I have this ghastly gut feeling that it's something more sinister, that Abigail is on the warpath?

Because, she reproved herself, you're paranoid. You're superstitious. You've been influenced too much by Anderson's view of his own mother. You give her supernatural powers. Now pull yourself together.

Nevertheless, she made another list: *People with an interest in knowing.* And at the top of the list, naturally, was Abigail Thorpe. If there were any possible way to trace Matthew's existence, Abigail the armor-plated martriarch would do it. But Marni, looking at her first list, felt reassured that there was no possible way. She couldn't exactly imagine Lady Abigail and one of Steve's hangers-on in the same

Back Bay living room swapping gossip on the Empress Abigail's ex-daughter-in-law.

Beneath Abigail, she wrote Anderson Thorpe III, her ex-husband. Poor Anderson. She didn't hold him guilty of anything except having Abigail for a mother, which was hardly his fault. Well, perhaps she held him slightly responsible for Geraint Finnbar, who brought a sense of uneasiness with him like a fog, but that was hardly Andy's fault either; in fact, the fault lay the other way around. It was Geraint who had introduced her to Andy. Anyway, Andy paid in spades for any emotional mayhem Geraint created.

She added Geraint's name to the list, since he had such a compulsion to know everything about everyone—for no sensible reason, that she could think of, except that to Geraint, knowledge was power. The power to make stinging dinner-table jokes. If Anderson knew anything, then Geraint would have wormed it out of him. But Anderson knew nothing, so she crossed Geraint's name off the list.

Poor Anderson.

She and Andy had an understanding; they met for dinner once a year on their wedding anniversary in April; she was fond of Andy. Sometimes she felt guilty for never telling him about Matthew, who had arrived just seven months after their formal separation. At the time, because the annulment had not come through, the risks and possible complications, not to mention the legalities, had meant it was out of the question. Perhaps the time had come to tell him, though the idea of a son would probably terrify Andy. Well, actually, what would terrify him was the idea of his mother knowing he had a son. A son more or less born out of wedlock, post wedlock, an "illegitimate" son. Just the same, perhaps it was time to take formal legal steps of protection, to come out of the closet as a mother.

Marni sighed. There was no one else to add to the list. There should have been her own father's name, but he'd died suddenly just before Matthew was born. Marni bit her lip. Poor Dad. He'd hoped for so much from her marriage. At the formal Ukrainian ceremony, he'd had tears in his eyes. "My child," he'd said. "My child." He'd had trouble speaking.

The shock of a failed marriage (she felt she had to explain to him the real reason), of the pending annulment, then Marni's pregnancy and her insistence on secrecy (a grandchild he couldn't talk about!) had all been too much for him. In the same month, Marni had lost a father and gained a son.

She breathed deeply. *Don't dwell on the losses.* Hold fast to good memories, true friends, the trusting eyes of Matthew.

So. If it really wasn't possible for Abigail to know anything (and it wasn't; it *wasn't*), then the midnight caller *had* to be some weirdo contact of Steve's. This could be dealt with.

She looked at her calendar for the day: Thursday, February 11, 1988. Between the 9:00 a.m. business meeting and the 11:00 a.m. meeting at City Hall, she penciled in two phone calls to be made.

Call Andy: call Ainsley.

Then she dialed Wilderness, Vermont, again.

"Eva? Is everything all right?"

"Marni, what *happened* last night?"

"Look, I don't want to talk about it over the phone. Tell me, are any of Steve's friends camping out in your woods at present?"

"Well, yes, as a matter of—"

"I thought so. Okay. I can't talk about it now, but something sick is going on."

"It's funny," Eva mused, "that you should say that—"

"Why?"

"Well, I don't know . . . Steve's been . . . Just two nights ago I said almost those very words to him. I said: *I feel as though something strange is going on.* It seems to me he's been very tense. But when I ask him, he says it's nothing. And something else—maybe it's nothing—there've been phone calls, and when I answer, the caller hangs up."

"I'm right then. It's one of your drifters. Can you be extremely careful? Listen, I think I can finish up business by noon tomorrow. I want to be out of Boston before the Friday afternoon traffic. I'll stay for the weekend, okay? Eva, can I speak to him?"

There was a sound of shuffling, then the voice of a five-year-old boy, a little diffident, a little shy. "Hi, Mommy."

"Oh Matthew," Marni said. "I do miss you."

2: Boston Mansions Inc.

When Marni arrived at her office on Newbury Street at nine the next morning, Roger Busch, her boss, was already chalking up new names on the board.

"Hi, gorgeous." He glanced up momentarily. "You look a bit peaky."

"Hi, Rog. Yeah. Bad night."

"Wha'd'you do? Dream that Valisi beat us to the Chestnut Street property?"

"Something like that," she said. "Bad dream, anyway." It didn't really seem much worse than that now; now that she'd analyzed it; now that she was here in her office with the old wall clock ticking away, Roger cocky as usual, everything where it should be, everything normal. And Matthew was safe, of course he was. She willed a fresh flicker of anxiety into stillness and watched the entries Roger was chalking in. "Hey!" Her eyebrows went up. "I don't believe it! A tenant for 108 Marlborough at last! Who pulled that off?"

Roger made a sweeping bow, all mock elegance. "Yours truly, in brilliant person."

"Mr. Amazing."

"Well," he said. "The problem was never finding interested tenants. The problem was the owner."

"Tell me about it," Marni groaned.

"Aha! You too tangled with the old lady, did you?"

"Bent so far backward, I got mud in my hair. Still didn't get anywhere."

"Takes a certain touch," Roger laughed.

"Ha. Takes a ladies' man, you mean. Takes smarm."

"Uh-oh. Jealousy showing."

It was true. Marni was grudgingly impressed by anyone who could unsnarl the owner problems. Owner problems at Boston Mansions Inc. meant owners who never needed money. They owned more real estate than they needed, and they owned far more money than they needed. When they were off in Aspen or Florida or Europe, they listed their Boston properties (Beacon Hill or Back Bay mansions and condominiums) with Roger or some other broker, to rent fully furnished on a short-term basis. Five hundred dollars and up per week. Not for the money. And certainly not for the prestige, which was generations thick in their blood. And not because they particularly *wanted* strangers living in their family space. Why, then? For security. Because high-paying gilt-edged tenants were protection against break-ins, and these owners often had valuable art collections in their houses. But of course they also had elaborate security systems, and usually a lifetime history of acting on whims. On Monday they wanted high-caliber tenants, on Tuesday they didn't. On Wednesday they worried because the alarm system might not be sufficiently foolproof and therefore they *should* have tenants, on Thursday an old friend from Venice called to say she was going to be in Boston for three days, so could Boston Mansions Inc. please explain to the incumbent tenant that he had six hours to get out. On Friday, the friend from Venice changed her mind, so could they please put the tenant back in?

Rental brokering for such people required the patience of a saint as well as ESP and supertact.

"So what'd you do, Rog?"

"Oh, you know, a little soft shoe, a little flattery. Hand-holder for the rich and discreetly famous, that's me. Got another two listings this week. Carte blanche for one of them. You know the Pinkertons?"

Marni raised her eyebrows. "The theater branch of the family? Or the supermarket branch?"

"The supermarket branch. Son number two just bought one of those huge brownstones on Commonwealth Avenue. He's having it rewired, then he's listing through me as long as I do the rest: new appliances, interior decorator, the works. Nice deal. What about you, Marni? Anything this week?"

"Yeah, one. Ninety-six Walnut Street, on the Hill."

Roger made a circle with his thumb and index finger. "That's my girl."

Marni narrowed her eyes. "*Girl?*" she challenged.

"Oops," he said. "Sorry. *Woman.* That's my number-one hot-shot woman."

"Your sexism is noted, but forgiven," Marni said. "At least you're trying." As she moved off toward her own office, she tossed over her shoulder: "I'm seeing Alonso and Jacobson from City Hall today. Taking them out to Jamaica Plain. Got another deal about to close out there, as a matter of fact. Fabulous old house. Got my renovating crew at the ready."

"Marni, Marni, totally barmy. You and your goodwill schemes!"

"Goodwill nothing. I just happen to be killing about three birds with one stone. You'll see. You'll come groveling."

"Yeah. When the moon turns blue." Roger shook his head and went on chalking entries onto the rental board. "Strategy meeting in ten minutes, remember."

"I know," she called from her office door. "By the way, seen the weather forecast?"

"No. Why? Groundhog show up late? Winter been canceled?"

"They're calling for blue moons."

"Yeah, yeah. Very funny. I can see the headlines, Marni: BUSINESS-WOMAN FOUND STABBED IN JAMAICA PLAIN—CASUALTY OF DRUG WARS, POLICE SAY."

Marni's dismissive laugh floated down the hallway.

There were eleven people around the table for the weekly strategy meeting, but Michael Lavan, legal counsel, had not yet arrived. Marni was conscious of this by the fact that she still felt relaxed. A certain amount of tension arrived with him, though she could not quite put her finger on the exact nature of that tension. Well, the main reason was obvious, of course, but somehow the main reason did not fully account for what was happening. It was this sense she got that behind his distance, his elaborate courtesy, there was something that felt like . . . well, outright hostility. (But how could it possibly be hostility? And if it wasn't, what was it? Hostility didn't make sense. It was illogical. If there was to be enmity, shouldn't it have been the other way around? After all, he was the one who'd intentionally practiced deception, not Marni. Perhaps this was the inevitable way men handled sexual rejection. Or perhaps it was all in her own mind? She just wished it would all go away, she wished she'd never spent those few weekends and nights . . .)

"Well," Roger said. "Late news should be good news. When Mike comes, we'll know if we've got Chestnut Street."

"No real risk, is there?" someone asked.

"Me, I don't jinx things by counting chickens," Roger said. "But if we don't get it, feathers are gonna fly."

He called the meeting to order, and the usual discussions began: properties being acquired, properties worth acquiring, properties worth a second look, renovation plans on properties recently purchased.

Roger had two simple rules: Buy cheap, sell high.

Expressed in fuller detail, this meant: Buy severely dilapidated buildings at throwaway prices, renovate up to luxury level, rent high on the fully furnished short-term market (to visiting consultants, visiting professors, circuit court judges, celebrity musicians and theater people in Boston for short-term stints). Just when the interiors and the new appliances are beginning to show the first signs of wear and tear, put the building on the market as an established investment property and sell high. Very high. Very, very high. Or the building could go condo, and they could sell it off floor by floor, $250,000 per one-bedroom unit, minimum.

Roger, who began just a decade ago with no college degree and a bank account of five thousand dollars (a down payment on a derelict building), had accumulated assets of several million dollars by this method.

The meeting's agenda moved on to the rental-brokerage business, which was not where the money lay, but where the prestige was. And prestige cast a subtle, enhancing glow on the rest of the business.

Staying in Boston? asked Roger's ads (in *Fortune*, in *The New*

Yorker, in the New York Times Magazine). Forget the blah, the ordinary, the run-of-the-mill luxury hotels. Be unique. Live the way Old Money lives, live in the dynastic homes of our founding families. Live in the mansions of Boston's Beacon Hill and the Back Bay. Fully furnished, down to the linen and the silverware. Short-term leases, by the week, by the month. Starting at $500 per week (not including brokerage fee).

Of course there were problems. Celebrity rock stars could pay a thousand a week without blinking, but this did not make them good tenants on Beacon Hill in a house whose walls were heavy with original art. Celebrity rock stars threw wild parties. Roger and his team had to be specialists in the matching up of appropriate tenant with appropriate space.

Roger looked at his watch, frowned, looked at the door. Everyone was waiting for Michael Lavan. Then they could get down to the item of serious business: the competition from Joe Valisi's Olde Pilgrim Realty. Olde Pilgrim, a newly formed upstart whose connection with New England heritage ran no further than its name and its intentions, was muscling in on Roger's territory.

"And when I say *muscling* in," Roger told his team, "I mean it. Those Johnny-come-latelies are getting nasty." There was a stir at the door, and Michael Lavan came in. "Ah. Been waiting for you, Mike. Are we going to get Chestnut Street or not?"

Roger did not for a moment believe there was any doubt about this, but he got a kick from the mock suspense, the momentous few seconds of waiting before another triumph.

"I'm afraid not," Michael said, taking a seat next to Roger. Michael's voice was very Harvard, very New England, as pleasing and elegant as a Sargent painting in Boston's Gardner Museum. Different from the other accents around the table, whose owners had put themselves through night schools and community colleges and the school of hard knocks. Perhaps it was Michael's voice that mesmerized everyone. There were a few seconds of silence while the faces around the table simply stared.

Roger blinked. "What?" he asked blankly.

"I'm afraid we didn't get it," Michael said.

Roger swore unprintably and banged a fist on the table. "Why not? Why the hell not?"

Michael said: "That's what we need to find out. Needless to say, I was very taken aback. The seller was extremely nervous, said he'd accepted another offer, wouldn't say whose. I dispatched one of our articling clerks to trace it through the deed registration. Olde Pilgrim, as you'd expect. There's no question Valisi strong-armed him. The question is how? And can we catch him out legally? He's smart and dangerous. And I'm beginning to think there's dangerous clout behind him."

"What do you mean?" Roger snapped.

"I don't really know what I mean. It's just that . . ." Michael looked somber and tapped a pen on the table. "I'd rather not say at this meeting," he said carefully.

"What the hell are you getting at?"

Marni raised her eyes then, startled. Everyone looked at Michael, who looked around the table slowly, from face to face, reading eyes. He said slowly: "There was something the seller's lawyer let slip. Something that gave me a shock." He paused. "He had privileged information on our financing structure." Michael looked significantly at Roger. "What that means," he said, "is that someone at this table is passing information to Valisi."

A gasp passed around the room like a small breeze.

"Not necessarily willingly," Michael added. "From the extreme nervousness of our potential client, my hunch is that Valisi is either employing, or is himself in the clutches of, an organization not known to shy off violence."

"Shit." Roger stared at Michael.

"You shouldn't be too surprised," Michael said. "Given the changes in your own personal worth over the past decade. Certain people notice things like that. In a way, you should take it as a compliment."

"Holy shit," Roger said.

"Exactly." Michael smiled very faintly and caught Marni's eyes. He was waiting for something from her. Appreciation? Awe? Or . . . or what?

"Has anyone here," Michael asked, "been put under pressure? Received threats? Intimidation? Anything like that?"

An abyss of panic suddenly opened up inside Marni, and she stared at her notes, clasped her hands so firmly together, under cover of the table, that the nails of one hand cut into the back of the other.

She heard a voice with a slight almost-lisp: *I can see . . . the blue floral pattern on your sheets . . .*

But this was ridiculous. There couldn't possibly be a connection because there was no possible way that Matthew's whereabouts (or even his existence) could be known to . . . to the kind of people for whom he might be a meaningless pawn in a deadly game for money and real estate and power.

Was there?

And what was the meaning of Michael's look? Why could she feel him *willing* her to look into his eyes?

Oh God, was it possible that *he.* . . . She remembered, suddenly, that moment when she had been about to tell him. Then she had thought better of it. But was it possible that she had said something unguarded over wine one night? Or in sleep?

No. Not possible. Marni took slow, deep breaths, clearing her head. She had never said a thing to him about Matthew, because she had wanted to be really sure what she felt about Michael first. And then chaos had come at them, so she'd never. . . . Really, really, she was getting paranoid. Her private life had nothing whatsoever to do with the power games of rival realty companies.

And what was Roger saying? She struggled to pay attention, to get her mind on track. Roger was rattled, no question about that. He was asking questions around the table, playing inquisitor, making each employee look into his eyes and answer.

"Marni?" Roger said. "Any pressures? Any threats?"

She could feel the sweat on her upper lip. Under the table, her knuckles turned white. "Rog," she said, "I'd rather die than fraternize with the enemy. My whole career is sewn up with yours, you know that."

"Yeah," he said. "I know that. But that wasn't the question. Any threats?"

"No threats," she said evenly, her knees turning weak. (Why was

Michael looking at her like that? She could see his stare from the edge of her eye.)

"Right," Roger said, moving on, completing the circuit. "Hell," he said, at the end of it. "All I can say is, if I find out that anyone who works for me is betraying me, I'll have him spiked on the Bunker Hill monument and barbecued on the State House lawn."

"Or her," Marni couldn't resist adding.

"Or her," Roger parroted sarcastically. "Shit, I'm no sexist. Any woman smart-ass enough to rat on me, I'll serve her balls up for jelly same as I would a man's."

Back in her own office after the meeting, Marni sensed the shadow of Michael Lavan in her doorway. She went on working.

"Marni," he said. "I had the odd feeling that you weren't being totally honest at the meeting."

She looked, then, uneasy again. This was the first time in weeks that Michael had spoken to her directly. He sat down across from her, his blue-gray eyes level with hers. They looked expressionless, but also . . . what? Sincere. There was the problem: *sincere*. He was putting on his sincere look, and for some reason it struck her as almost ominous.

There was something about that whole crowd, she thought. It wasn't that Michael had ever been, so far as she knew, in any sense close to Geraint or to Anderson Thorpe III, her ex-husband, but they had all been at prep school and Harvard together. And all three seemed to be equal parts shimmer and deception. Well, with Anderson it was different; she didn't consider him dishonest, exactly. Not in the same way. Their marriage was a fiasco, but she didn't blame Andy. Not really (though she did blame Abigail a little, his mother, watchdog of the Mayflower bloodlines). No, she didn't blame Andy. But it was not the kind of mistake you wanted to make twice. It was unnerving that she could have fallen for Michael, and *then* found out he was at school with Andy; and then found out how much he had in common with Andy and Geraint both. It must be that prep schools turned out clones.

"You seemed . . . evasive to me," Michael said.

"Really?"

"If you're under some sort of pressure," Michael said, "I'm sympathetic and I'd like to help. But I wouldn't want you to rely on what has happened between us to protect you if you're . . . if it's you who's . . ."

There it is, she thought suddenly. That's what makes me uneasy. It's the covert nature of his hostility. The suggestion of veiled threat. And she thought with a shock: of course, he knows what my sheets look like.

She thought back to the distraught phone call she'd had from his wife. Two, three months ago, was it?

"What are your intentions with my husband?" an icy voice had asked.

"Pardon?"

"This is Mary Lavan. My husband has told me about the way you've been throwing yourself at him. I want you to know it's over."

Marni was too confused, too shocked to speak. Throwing herself at him? This from the man who'd been ardently pursuing her for months? Who'd swamped her caution with phone calls, flowers, business trips together, and yes (don't think about that now), it had been wonderful. Yes, after the years of rigid self-protection, of not letting herself even think about involvements, she'd begun to let her defenses down.

She couldn't think. Her mind was on a roller coaster somewhere in the middle of a storm. Mary Lavan's voice was going on and on, growing more and more shrill, faltering here and there, sometimes getting close to what sounded like a sob.

Marni thought with a sudden flash of empathy: This is another woman in shock.

"Mrs. Lavan," she had said as neutrally as she could manage. "I'm truly sorry. I didn't realize. . . . He told me that for both of you the marriage had been dead for years. He said he was in the process of getting a divorce."

"That's not true," Mary Lavan said. "He never said that to you at all. It's not true. We've been together for years and years, we have two children, it's me he loves." Then she began to sob. "You slut," she screamed. "You slut."

I don't believe this is happening, Marni thought. These conversations don't take place in real life.

She'd never seen herself as the other woman. She didn't like the role. "Mrs. Lavan," she said, alarmed now because the hysteria was rising. "I'm sure he—"

"Tramp!" Mrs. Lavan sobbed. "I can promise you this, I don't care what I have to do, I don't care what I have to say, he'll never leave me. It's over, do you understand? It's over."

"Yes," Marni said quietly. "I can promise you that, Mrs. Lavan. It's over."

She'd been stunned when Michael dropped by as usual that evening, as though nothing had happened.

"Michael," she had said, quietly, dully, resisting his arms. "How could you be so dishonest?"

"What do you mean?"

"Your wife called me today."

"What!" He was thunderstruck. "Shit. How the hell did she even know your name? She has antennae like you wouldn't believe. Sometimes I could swear she has ESP."

"I think spouses usually know, Michael. I don't think it's so hard to tell. Why did you lie to me?"

"I didn't lie to you. She means nothing to me."

"About the divorce, I mean."

"You don't understand," he said. He was pacing, pacing, trembling. "It's the children. You have no idea of the. . . . My wife is given to many forms of subtle blackmail." He looked like a frightened little boy. "There's no telling what she might. . . . I have to go." He practically ran down the hall to the elevator. From her window, she watched the way his car bucked from the curb.

The next day at the office, he said, "I've convinced her she was overreacting, that you're just a business associate. She's feeling pretty badly embarrassed now, but we'll have to cool it. She has spies at the office. We'll have to rely on conferences, occasional weeks away."

She'd stared at him in disbelief. "Michael," she said. "That's simply not the kind of relationship I'm interested in."

He'd taken her face between his hands almost violently. "This isn't something we can just throw away."

She had removed his hands. "I did care, Michael," she sighed. "Unfortunately."

"And I'm crazy about you," he said. "So as long as we're careful, the world's our oyster."

She had looked at him then and thought: This man is a total stranger. I didn't know him. I don't know him at all. Not at all.

It seemed to her that the fluorescent lighting in the office came right through him, that he was hollow, that he was a charming shell around a nothingness. And yet those business trips, that last night and then breakfast together. . . . She said quickly: "Don't make it any harder, Michael. Let's part as friends."

"Don't be childish, Marni." The harsh light seemed to reveal something she hadn't noticed before, something in the way he pressed his lips together. "Let's be adults," he said, taking her wrists in his hands. Perhaps it was accidental that he twisted her arms as he pulled her toward himself. "And realists," he added.

She could only think: Dr. Jekyll and Mr. Hyde.

"Michael," she'd said, wanting to lock herself away somewhere private, in some bathroom, where she could cry. "This doesn't do anything for my . . ." She wanted to say: I've lost respect for you, don't make it worse. But she floundered: "You can't . . . I can't . . . I won't pretend I don't hurt like hell. But it's absolutely over."

She saw the shade fall across his eyes. Then he had left without speaking.

Since then, there had been no reference whatsoever to the trips away together, to the last night together on Beacon Hill, to anything. They had been polite strangers. On Michael's side, *barely* polite.

"I wouldn't want you to rely on what has happened between us to protect you," he was saying now, silkily, "if you're . . . if it's you who's . . ."

"Michael, I have difficulty understanding why you are so hostile toward me."

"Hostile?" he said coolly. "I think you're projecting, Marni."

She raised her eyebrows. "I don't believe this. Okay, let it go." She swiveled in her chair, turning away from him, then swiveled back. "I feel a very healthy competition against Olde Pilgrim, and I can promise you I have nothing to do with the leak." She looked him square in the eyes. "And I find it sad, Michael, that you consider it necessary to pay such an insult."

"My wife is a very good judge of character," he said.

She couldn't believe he was bringing his wife into this.

"My wife," he said, "can tell a great deal from a voice on the phone. And when you called her—"

"When I called her?"

"A rather vicious thing to do, I have to say."

Marni simply stared.

"And it is my wife's opinion that you are a pathological liar."

Marni put out a hand to steady herself, to find out if the table was solid, if the world had gone upside down. What was he so scared of, or so angry about, that he needed to rewrite the so-recent past? She recalled Mary Lavan's desperate threat: *I don't care what I have to do, I don't care what I have to say. . . .* Was it loss of custody of the children? she wondered. Was that the threat? When children were involved, people never got free from each other, never fully disentangled themselves, she knew that only too well.

People need to concoct stories to save face, she thought. Then they need to convince themselves that the stories are true.

"Michael," she said quietly. "Would you please leave my office now?"

"Not until I've said what I came to say. You seemed extremely tense at the meeting."

Marni raised her eyebrows slightly but went on making notes on her scratch pad.

"Look at me, Marni."

"Michael," she said curtly, not looking. "I'm not in your pocket, you know."

"Hell hath no fury," he laughed.

She *was* furious then. She did look at him. She felt astonishment, then a moment of pure and intense dislike.

Something curious happened. He leaned over the desk toward her. "I love it," he said thickly, "when you're mad like that. You give off sparks. Remember that night I chased you around the hotel room?"

For a second, Marni's bodily responses took over. A sharp memory of passion played fleetingly across her nerve ends; she felt fluid, languid. Sexually hungry.

But then . . . *God! Did I blab anything that night? Did I mention Matthew? No. No. I'm certain I didn't.*

She said shakily: "Feelings do change, Michael."

His eyes were bright with sexual invitation for a moment longer, but she turned away.

He said coldly: "Yes. They certainly do. Especially when you find out it's just another tramp who's been throwing herself at you."

That Michael and this Michael, she thought, bewildered. Dr. Jekyll and Mr. Hyde. Why couldn't ex-lovers be civil to one another?

"So we're back to my question," he said smoothly. "Are you absolutely sure no one put pressure on you this week? Threatened you?"

Marni's mouth felt dry, but she looked at him and frowned a little, then shrugged to imply that she couldn't imagine what he was talking about.

"I wouldn't try to play heroics or go solo with this crowd, Marni," he warned.

Once he had left her office, Marni felt such a vacuum, such vulnerability, that she wanted to race after him, turn the clock back, accept his terms (cheating in secret), babble on about Matthew and Wilderness, Vermont, and death threats and . . .

But no. It never paid to rush into trusting people.

I don't understand men, she thought. I don't understand them at all.

So instead she made her phone calls. She called Anderson, her ex-husband, at his Antiques Gallery. She didn't connect with Andy himself, of course (he was hardly ever actually there), but she arranged with his secretary to have dinner with him that evening.

Then she called Ainsley's office, and made an appointment for the following morning.

She had an irresistible urge to call Vermont again, to talk to Matthew. She began dialing, but paused after the third digit. Suppose her calls were being monitored? (Suppose Michael or Michael's wife . . .? Oh, stop it! Paranoia, Marni, pure paranoia!) But suppose there was someone who was trying to find out where Matthew was? Suppose someone was tracking down the area codes she dialed? She hung up. She checked that all the necessary documents were in her briefcase and walked to the Exeter Street garage where she kept her car during the day.

At a pay phone on the way to the garage, she stopped and called Vermont. Eva answered.

"Marni? He's down at the pond with Deszo. I can see them from here. You want me to go and get him?"

"No, no," Marni said. "As long as everything is okay."

"I wish you'd tell me what all this is about," Eva said. "You're making me dreadfully nervous."

"Yeah, well. I'm very nervous myself. I had a death threat about Matthew."

"My God!"

"Yeah. Eva, I don't like to say this, but I think it's got to be one of Steve's hangers-on."

"Oh, sweet Jesus," Eva said. She sighed a long, audible sigh. "Marni, I've got stuff to tell you, too."

"What kind of stuff?"

"Not now. When you get here. But don't worry, I won't let him out of my sight."

"Thanks, Eva. See you tomorrow evening."

She got her car and headed for City Hall to pick up Alonso and Jacobson.

3: Dream House

Alonso sat in the front seat of Marni's Pontiac Firebird, Jacobson sat in the back. Marni took them out via the Fenway and Jamaicaway. Taking Washington Street or Huntington Avenue would have been shorter, but she didn't want to depress them before they got there. She wanted the effect to be sharp and sudden.

As they passed Jamaica Pond, Jacobson said something about skating there when he was ten years old. Good, Marni thought. Get them nostalgic about the inner city before it went to seed. She skirted the Arnold Arboretum, its vistas beautiful even under February snow, and Jacobson sighed. "My mother's parents used to live out here," he said. "Used to take me horse riding in Franklin Park."

Alonso grunted. "Need an armored car to be safe in Franklin Park. These days, I mean."

"I know it," Jacobson sighed. "I know it."

"Franklin Park coming up," Marni said. She glided out of the rotary, and they emerged from the slightly decaying graciousness of the Jamaicaway houses. Even before the treetops of the arboretum dropped from sight, another country announced itself. A couple of cars stripped to the axles slumped at the park gates, all their windows smashed. Five teenagers, three boys and two girls, were stuffed into one of the cars like sardines, their ghetto blaster like a sacred object on the altar of the hood. The kids wore ratty parkas and huddled together for warmth. A reefer, which they made no attempt to hide, was being passed around. One of the boys and one of the girls were white. The white girl's hairstyle was short and punk, lethally spiked.

Marni curved away from the park and glided under the shadow of

24

the Washington Street elevated train tracks. The effect was dramatic, depressing, frightening. It was dark and gloomy under the tracks. Ugly one-story box buildings with garish signs announced: Auto Bodywork. Dry Cleaning. Chinese Laundry. The sidewalks were crowded with harried welfare mothers juggling toddlers and groceries. There were girls in high heels and black stockings and very short leather skirts, whose thighs must have been numb in the February air. They wore parkas, and paced up and down and breathed steam and hugged themselves as though warm arms might somehow send warmth down to their long, sexy legs. They wore poignantly innocent plastic butterfly clips in their hair. One girl, who couldn't have been more than thirteen years old, wore a pink ribbon. Their pimps, cozy in parked cars, kept watch, waiting for the factory shifts to change, for the workers to come down the steps from the Orange Line elevated subway stops, waiting for those tired men who needed a quick, cheap thrill to make the day bearable. And then there were the drug pushers and con men and drunks and unemployed teenagers hanging out. Loud music came blasting from all directions, bouncing back from the steel girders above, ricocheting, echoing, deafening, a myriad sound tracks clashing. Overhead, the trains thundered by, the ground vibrated. Grime fell like rain. The snow was dirty. There was a sense of dangerous, frenetic energy fizzing about under a mushroom cloud of despair.

"Jesus!" Alonso said, and shivered.

Marni stopped for a red light, and a large, battered Chevy drew alongside, its four occupants staring at Marni's Firebird. From the sidewalks, too, there was a gallery of eyes, all hostile.

Jacobson said quietly: "I feel very conspicuously white."

"I don't know," Alonso said, depressed. "I don't know. We've given them Headstart. Schools. Busing. What'll it take? Who'd live in a place like this?"

"I used to," Marni said. "I grew up in Jamaica Plain."

"God!" Alonso was startled.

"It wasn't always like this," Marni said. "Oh sure, even then it was for immigrants, blacks, the poor. But it was a good neighborhood."

"Yes," Jacobson said. "I remember. When I was a kid, my grandparents . . ."

"It could be different," Marni said. "Things could change."

She turned off Washington into Green, crossed Forest Hills, headed back toward the boundary of Franklin Park, then turned into a short, dead-end side street, Park Lane.

"People used to have potted geraniums on their front porches and little vegetable gardens at the back," she said. "They used to whitewash the porch railings every spring."

She was moving slowly now past derelict triple deckers. Some of the windows were boarded up, there was trash in the street and battered garbage cans that were stuck in snowbanks till spring. Abandoned cars stripped of anything that could be sold for quick drug money were buried up to the door handles in unshoveled snow that had settled into a form of pack ice. And then, in the cul-de-sac at the end of the street, rising like a fantasy before the windshield, was Marni's trump card.

"Holy shit!" Alonso, in the front seat, saw it first.

The huge old triple decker was newly painted, crisp white clapboard with blue shutters at the windows. Every spindle and finial of the intricate veranda railing had been replaced, the cornices over the bay windows repaired to perfection. It was a gracious dowager empress of a house.

"Well, gentlemen," Marni said. "I want you to see what can be done." She leaned on her wheel and looked up lovingly through her windshield. "Six months ago," she said, "this house was a shambles. It was divided into six apartments, fifteen people were living in it, the furnace gave out, the pipes froze and burst, and an absentee landlord wanted to unload it quickly rather than do any repairs. So I got it for a song, with next to nothing down. I'd like to show you inside."

Alonso said nervously: "Is it safe here?"

Marni shrugged. "Well, my car was stolen from this very spot a few months back, but the police found it again ten blocks away. Just kids, joyriding. The black schoolteacher next door was mugged last month, but it was quick: a knife at her throat, her purse snatched, no physical

Now I'm down on my luck.
Can you spare a buck?
God bless."

"Under the lines," Marni said, "it was signed: Joseph Lucyk. I couldn't believe it. Joseph Lucyk! This man right here." She hugged him again. "Maybe Joseph should tell you the next bit."

"Yeah." Joseph smiled. "Well, I was so cold, I had one thought going off like a siren in my mind. Next dollar, I'd be into McDonald's and buy three coffees, one after the other, drink them slow so I could sit in the warm. And then there's this crazy woman, crying she is, babbling something, talking about her dad and the old days in Jamaica Plain and then I see, *Jesus, Mary, and Joseph*, it's little Marni Verstak, with the exact same eyes as when she was in her white First Communion dress and veil at St. Aloysius. Last time I see her, she was wearing satin and lace and getting married at that very same church."

"Joseph and my dad emigrated together," Marni explained. "Back in . . . when was it, Joseph?"

"Late thirties, we were kids together on the boat. Worked at Nelson Tire Factory together for forty years. Then Marni's dad died, and I still worked there till the place folded two years ago." Joseph rubbed a hand across his eyes. "Place folds when you're my age," he said, "means trouble. Pension down the tubes. My wife died ten years ago. No kids. For a year, I paid the rent from my savings, pounding pavement, looking for work. What can you get when you're sixty years old? Then my savings gave out, and I been on the streets, living in the subways. Been doing that for a year when Marni found me."

"I couldn't believe it," Marni said. "I was shocked. Outraged. I got a room for Joseph. I tried to get work for him. Then I realized he was right. You can't get work for a sixty-year-old man. And he told me there were plenty like him on the streets, and younger too. Layoffs, bad luck, bad timing, it's a downward spiral. Once you can't pay the rent for a month, you're on the skids. And once you don't have a phone or an address, you can't get anywhere with job ads or employment agencies. They won't touch you. It's a nightmare. And with bad luck, it can happen to almost anyone."

"Yeah," Alonso and Jacobson agreed, though privately each thought it couldn't possibly happen to him; that, in fact, there must surely be something a little . . . *irresponsible*, a little careless, about anyone to whom such a thing happened.

Marni led Alonso and Jacobson into the pristine kitchen and made coffee. "I thought and thought," she said. "I tried to harangue Roger, head of my company, into giving Joseph a job. Rog said I was a bleeding heart, impractical."

Marni took a deep breath. "I was taking Joseph for a drive through the old neighborhood when we saw this house with a For Sale sign, and I suddenly got my brilliant idea. Joseph said he could get a team together just from the doorways and subway shelters around Copley Square, there were men wanting to work, men desperate to work their butts off just to feel like human beings again. And he was right. This construction team works harder than any construction crew you ever saw. Now, I did have to sweet-talk a bank manager for *hours* to get a bridging loan. I put Joseph's team to work. In return for their labor, they got to live in this house. Now I've got a potential buyer, a black storekeeper runs a deli on Washington Street, we went by it under the elevated tracks. He wants to buy if he can qualify for mortgage money. He's borderline as far as the banks are concerned. He'll live on the first floor and rent the two top floors, reasonable rents for blue-collar families. We've got the mathematics all worked out between us. If he buys, I've covered costs, made enough for down payments on two more properties. We'll expand, Joseph will cruise the streets for more workers, and we'll get to work renovating.

"Now." She leaned across the kitchen table and looked from Alonso to Jacobson. "If the city came in as a partner, put up venture capital, held the mortgages, gave mortgages to people who don't quite meet bank requirements but are very hard workers, very committed, very much want a house . . . if the city would do stuff like that, we'd be giving shelter and jobs to the homeless, renovating a neighborhood, fostering civic pride. What do you say?"

She could see votes and caution, in equal parts, dancing across their eyes.

"It's a dream, a dream," Jacobson said. "Great for public relations.

neighborhoods around. Hey, maybe I should go straight to the governor. It wouldn't hurt Dukakis's campaign, would it?"

"Yeah." Roger was not really listening. "You're keeping a client waiting."

"Who is it?"

"Forget his name. Some sort of connection with Michael, I think he said. Looked kind of familiar. Sure I've seen him on TV or in the *Globe* or somewhere. Very Beacon Hill except for the pink bow tie and the walking stick. Too flashy for the Hill. Must be Cambridge."

Marni should have known. A bow tie and a walking stick? Who else could it have been? But then again, context was everything, and how could she have been expecting Geraint Finnbar to show up here? It was part of his trademark to be supremely unpredictable. Always to take by surprise.

At any rate, she was certainly caught off guard when she saw him.

"Geraint! What on earth brings you here?"

"Fair lady," he said, with a sweeping bow. "*You* bring me here. I'd go to the ends of the earth for you any day of the week, as well you know." He reached for her hand and kissed the tips of her fingers. She laughed with slightly self-conscious nervousness. Although, for herself, it evoked uneasiness rather than pleasure, she was conscious of Geraint's dangerous charm. For most people—of both sexes—Geraint functioned as the flame does for the moth.

Each time, Marni thought, you could feel the singeing of your wing tips.

Each time he showed up, she felt uneasy. Profoundly uneasy. Each time it was a riddle she had to solve. She had to locate again the source of her distrust. It was as though Geraint had the power to cast spells so that when anyone was actually with him, that person forgot—or simply did not care—why misgivings had ever fluttered about.

Marni thought of Geraint as a reincarnation of Oscar Wilde. Everyone thought of him that way. At any party, a crowd clustered around him within minutes just to hear the throwaway one-liners, the laughs, the latest deliciously vicious gossip. He was a man who could make a black velvet opera cape and a satin bow tie seem perfectly normal and appropriate in the late 1980s and on the subway. Or wherever he chose to wear them, for that matter. If Geraint were to wear his "costume" to a picnic, or a clambake, it would seem just right. And under the cape was a superbly charming and somewhat ruthless . . . what? A reflection of a man in a costume.

When you saw Geraint, you thought of the endless stream of lovers of both sexes. You heard the stories of suicides, you read veiled references to the depression and madness of rejected short-term partners (famous people, artists, writers, singers, film stars) in such places as *Vanity Fair*, and you thought of that old ballad about the demon lover. And still you felt a little buzz of excitement when he dropped by or called or sent flowers, because . . . well, because he brought snap and crackle and the unexpected in his wake.

Nevertheless, Marni could never understand why so many people fell so disastrously in love with him. Certainly she had trouble understanding Andy's addiction, since it so regularly made him miserable. Geraint was a charmer, he was fun, he was intelligent, he knew everything there was to know about antiques and the art world and society gossip, but he could only play one note. She suspected that if she had a chance to tap on his forehead, she would hear an echo. There was layer after layer of elegance and wit, and then there was a void.

Well, there was just one other thing: an occasional slight wandering of one eye, like an incipient cast. And Marni suspected it was this little flaw in the surface perfection that lured so many people in. What did that tiny defect seem to promise? Secret vulnerability, a hidden life? And each fly in Geraint's web was flattered into believing he or she might hold the key to the mystery of a possibly tragic and fragile inner sanctum. Then the trap snapped shut. Then Geraint injected those high flyers with something that rendered them helpless, he sucked out their juices and left a shell dangling from the guy ropes of his web. It was not so much, Marni thought, that Geraint was immoral. (You might as well call a rock immoral for falling on someone's head.) It was just that a whole dimension was missing from him. The only safe stance with regard to falling rocks and to people like Geraint was to stay out of their way.

She felt suddenly warm toward Geraint. Perhaps after all there was something behind the hollowness. She felt as though the key had been placed in her hands. "Oh Gerry, that's so. . . . It's a lovely thing to do. Andy will love it. I'm having dinner with him tonight, by the way."

"Yes, I know."

"Oh." Surprise, surprise. (The thing was, she *was* always taken by surprise. Why did so much trivia matter to him?)

He wagged an admonitory finger at her. "Geraint knows everything. Always. Including the fact that you've been playing naughty games with Michael, and his sad little wife is quite distraught. She had a little cry on my shoulder." He put on his sagely woebegone look. "I gave what comfort I could."

I'll bet you did, Marni thought. "*Honestly,*" she said, shaking her head. "You people."

"Dear me." Geraint lifted his eyebrows dramatically. "You people? What *can* you mean? I hope that you don't mean to include a real-estate lawyer in my inner circle. It's true that Michael went to school with us, but he was never quite *of* us, you know. Always a trifle *déclassé*. That's why he married Mary. It's her family money he married, surely you understood that?"

"I know nothing about her," Marni said, dismissing the subject. (Except for her voice, her sobbing, she thought. Except that she's frightfully unhappy.) "I know almost nothing about Michael, for that matter. And I'm not interested."

"Not even in the fact that he made a joke about you at a dinner party last week?" Geraint's eyes glittered. "Did you know that?"

"No." Marni's eyes prickled.

"He likes to bring the past into line," Geraint smiled.

But it was just as likely, she thought, that this was purely an invention of Geraint's. She said levelly: "And what of *your* past, Geraint?"

Geraint was far too urbane to miss a beat. "What indeed?" he said archly. "And what of our several *futures*, dear lady? Which brings me to the fact that you and I need to have a little talk. About the matter you're planning to discuss with Anderson. . . ."

Marni stared at him, all her unease, all her nervousness rushing back. "What matter?" she asked.

Geraint looked her steadily in the eyes. "*You* know," he said, and it seemed to her that Matthew stood between them, that a road map leading to Wilderness, Vermont, was spread in the air above her desk, with flashing red arrows pointing to her endangered son. But this was crazy. Totally crazy. There was no possible way, it was not remotely possible that Geraint could. . . . (Unless Abigail did know, and told Anderson, who would tell Geraint . . . who helplessly told Geraint *everything*. But she was certain that Abigail didn't know. That the midnight caller—*was* there a call? or did she dream it?—that if there was a midnight caller, it was some two-bit blackmailer loosely attached to Steve.)

"Your hands are trembling," Geraint said solicitously, taking them in his. "I just wanted to suggest—" it seemed to Marni that the air was fogged with quiet menace "—that it might be wise to be discreet. As you yourself have just said, needless cruelty to Andy is upsetting. Much as you might doubt me, I also hate to see Andy hurt. So I don't think it's a good idea to be giving him disturbing news, do you?"

Marni felt as if she were going crazy. For a moment she had the unnerving sense that Geraint could read her thoughts. She almost said: "You don't think he'll take it well? The knowledge that he has a son?" But that's crazy, *crazy*, she told herself. "I'm afraid I don't know what you're talking—"

"Or his mother, the lovely Abigail," Geraint said. "We certainly wouldn't want to upset *her*, would we?"

She stared at him, baffled, nervous. He lifted an index finger toward her face and ran it lightly across her brows, down her nose, around her lips, and she stood there, frightened, bewildered, helpless in his web. "Ah Marni, Marni," he sighed, concentrating the blue energy of his eyes on hers. "Why do you hold out on me? You know we'll become lovers eventually, it's fated. There's absolutely nothing you can do about it."

A very powerful bodily chemistry moved with Geraint like an aura. How else could anyone explain why Marni's breath was turning ragged? He's *obnoxious*, she thought, furious, as she went on standing

Marni stared at him, seeing nothing. Geraint's eyes seemed like headlamps at night, blurred at the edges, blinding. Marni tried to read them. They made her own eyes water. They seemed to her full of warning and guarded menace. At last she said, stupidly: "Joseph Lucyk."

"Ah. Joseph Lucyk. The Ukrainian family tree? A skeleton in the family closet?" Geraint tapped his forehead. "Joseph Lucyk. Lucyk. Hmm. Rings a bell. Old friend of your father's, wasn't he?"

She said mechanically, as though answering an exam question: "He was working on a house I'm renovating. He's just been stabbed to death."

"How awful," Geraint said. "How . . . " His face resembled that of someone who has accidentally bitten into a lemon. "How *ugly*. Well, I won't keep you. You'll have matters to attend to." At the door, he paused. "That really is awful. I'm most dreadfully sorry. But then," he shook his head regretfully, "Park Lane is such an *unsavory* street these days."

It wasn't until after he'd gone that Marni asked herself how he knew the house was on Park Lane. Then she thought, well, from Michael Lavan, no doubt. Or from Michael's wife. It hasn't been a secret, my Jamaica Plain dream.

5: Nothing Quite Adds Up

When the police called her office, Marni's first reaction was panic. "I can't go to the morgue," she said. "I'm sorry, I can't. I just can't."

There was a second's pause, as though the officer had been winded by the vehement rush of her fear. Then he said: "There's no need, ma'am." It was a gentle voice, soothing, a voice not unfamiliar with breaking ghastly news to parents, wives, families. "The body was identified at the scene of death. A fellow worker, Ron Wells. Name mean anything?"

"Yes, he works for me," Marni said weakly. "I'm sorry, officer, for my . . . I'm in shock. Joseph Lucyk. . . . He was an old friend of my father's. I can't believe he's gone. It's only two hours since I was talking to him. It just doesn't seem *possible.*"

"It's always like that," the police officer sighed. "I'm really sorry, ma'am. Really sorry. These scumbags, life doesn't mean shit to them."

Scumbags. It wasn't a word she would use, but right now she felt grateful to have someone express her anger. Right now, she hated those kids. Hated them. Someone as gentle as Joseph, as harmless, someone who'd had a life as rough as any life those kids had had, who'd arrived on a boat with nothing, worked hard all his life, and been turned out on the streets in his sixties. It was unfair. *Unfair.* She wanted to scream and sob.

"Ma'am?"

"Yes. I'm sorry, officer. I'm having trouble . . ."

"I understand that, ma'am. Thing is, we were wondering if we could talk to you. I know this'll be difficult, but I'm sure you . . . See, the

41

"I work hard," she said. "Had some bad times along the way. I sure don't want to lose it all again."

McCarthy's eyes were suddenly sharp, focused on her. "Why'd you say that?"

"Well, I mean . . . the threats." (She could have kicked herself for saying it.) "I mean, our company lawyer has made us all a bit paranoid, I think. And Joseph's death. It won't be good for my project."

"How not good?"

So she explained. About Alonso and Jacobson. About her dream for her old neighborhood. "That neighborhood," she said. "I grew up there. Joe Lucyk lived there for forty years. We lived just a few blocks from that very street. I can't believe . . ." The full force of what had happened hit her again, and she buried her face in her hands.

"Ma'am," Boise said. "Maybe this is where you can help. The thing is, kids do this kinda thing in packs. We know the packs. Ghetto kids, white, black, Hispanic, don't make no difference. They work territories. They use stolen cars, then they dump the cars. They take the cash, they throw the wallets, the pocketbooks, the carrybags down some drain, in a trash can. Seventy percent we get back, with just the cash gone. Don't even bother about the credit cards anymore.

"Now, some ways this case is the usual. For example, the deceased just got cash from the Baybank machine. We found the machine receipt in his pants pocket, hadn't put it in his wallet even. Took out forty bucks fifteen minutes before he was killed. Very small account. Balance showed only a hundred dollars."

"He was so proud of that account," Marni said sadly. "He'd just opened it. He'd been without one for several years, living on the streets. But I don't pay the men very much. It's payment in kind, you see. They live in the house they're fixing. I hired them right off the street, they were homeless."

"Yes, ma'am. So Ron Wells explained. Well, like I was saying, kids watch those machines all the time. A lot of muggings connected to bank machines. Now, what's very strange," McCarthy said, "this woman in the house facing where it happened. She's nursing her baby when she hears the scream. She watches from the window, she's too scared to go out." He pauses apologetically. "That's the way it is, ma'am. What would anyone do, with a baby? Makes no sense to run out."

"Sure," Marni said, feeling sick, sympathizing with the frightened mother, feeling furious with her. (If she'd run out, mightn't Joe . . .?)

"See, afterwards she says there's something, but she can't remember. Something about the car. Very fancy, too fancy for a stolen car in J.P., but she doesn't know car makes. And then she remembers what's bothering her. It's not a kid driving the car. It's a white man. He stays behind the wheel and watches while the kids get out and do their thing.

"And another thing. There were kids hanging out in a car wreck at the end of the street."

"Yes," Marni said, leaning forward. "I remember them. They were there when I took Alonso and—"

"Took off when they heard the police sirens. But then they drifted back and volunteered some information. See, their territory had been invaded, and they didn't like it. Didn't like the idea of taking someone else's heat. So they told us—the kids who did it weren't from that area. They didn't know those kids. Which is very unusual, ma'am."

"And then," Boise said, "we got another witness, six blocks away, down by the subway, saw a white man in a BMW let a bunch of kids out and drive off. Sounds like our man."

"Very unusual," McCarthy said. "Maybe means nothing, maybe not."

"Maybe means what?" Marni asked.

"Well, Joseph Lucyk was your foreman, right? Anyone want to stop work on that house?"

"I think this is something Michael Lavan should know about," she said. "I think you should talk to him and Roger. Roger Busch. It's his company."

"If you think of anything, ma'am," they said as they left.

Then the *Boston Globe* called her. Jeff Smith, reporter for city affairs and politics, had had a tip from a councilman. Heard something interesting was going on. Could he do an interview for a story on her plans for inner-city neighborhoods?

Marni hesitated. Would it do any good to offset the murder with a story on urban renaissance dreams? Probably not. In fact, it would

He cleared his throat. "Ms. Verstak, this stabbing. . . . From experience . . . uh, it was an old friend, I believe? Yes, well, that's the . . . you'll be more in a state of shock than you realize. You'll find yourself doing odd, uh, impulsive . . . tears and so on, maybe crazy things. . . . Don't be hard on yourself when you feel as though, you know. . . ." He sighed, and paused for a couple of reflective puffs on his pipe. "Happens when violence arrives in a life like a Halloween trick." He looked directly into her eyes. "Hits hardest at people who are used to thinking they have everything under control." When he half-smiled like that, there were crinkle lines around his eyes.

"Well," he said. "I should get down to business and explain why I'm here. The governor has set up something called the Special Drug Task Force. We investigate everything, especially homicide, naturally, that appears to be drug-related. Establishing patterns, strategies."

He leaned toward her. "This stabbing . . . it's not just an ordinary kids' thing. The local officers explained?"

She nodded.

"We've talked to your company lawyer, what's his name? Lavan."

She waited.

"It could be," he said, "that this company, and perhaps you personally, have been accidentally caught up in something." He gestured vaguely to illustrate the something—a cobwebby, sinister thing.

Their eye contact was total. Neither moved, or seemed to breathe, for seconds.

"I just want you to know," he said, "that if you should come under any sort of pressure, or if you receive any threats, you have my personal assurance of confidence and protection."

"Thank you, Sergeant Murphy."

"Is there anything you might want to tell me now?"

She looked into his eyes, and did trust him. The middle-of-the-night calls and the threat to Matthew formed themselves into words just below her larynx, but when they tried to rise to her lips there was some barrier. It was as though fear stuffed her entire mouth like a gag. What if the point of the threats had nothing to do with drug and real-estate warfare, but were designed to make her reveal Matthew's whereabouts?

She said softly: "No, there's nothing I want to.... Not ... not now."

He did not release her eyes. He seemed to know exactly what she meant, to read the words below her words. He nodded slowly and handed her a card. "If you need me," he said, "call this number."

He got up to leave, and they shook hands. No, not exactly shook hands. Part of her mind, a clockwork, analytical part, decided: it would be more correct to say that he took her hand in his. There was something curious and yet faintly familiar about the gesture. Perhaps they maintained contact for a second longer than was usual.

At the door, he turned back and pointed to the Ukrainian icon. "Very beautiful," he said. "The techniques were handed down through generations of the same family for centuries, did you know that? Puts a lot of history in one frame, doesn't it?"

This man is a homicide detective in Boston? she thought with amazement. A man who makes drug busts?

She went on sitting at her desk, suspended in a daydreaming peacefulness, looking at the icon her father had left her, forgetting to ask Carol to hold her calls. It was probably only minutes before the phone rang again, and she picked up the receiver without thinking. "Mary?" a man's voice asked.

"*Marni*," she corrected. "Marni Verstak. Can I help you?"

"How odd," the voice said. "I always thought it was *Mary* and Joseph. And Luke and John and *Matthew*."

"What? Who *is* this?"

"Ah," the caller said. "Someone who keeps an eye on Matthew."

She heard the faint suggestion of lisp on the *s* sounds, then the click. She did not notice, as she frantically began to dial Eva's number, that she was biting her lip so hard it was bleeding. Halfway through the dialing, she stopped and looked jumpily about, in case the walls had eyes, in case Geraint was reading her thoughts.

Be calm, she told herself. Think.

She dialed the front office. "Carol," she said urgently. "Is Sergeant Murphy still there?"

She went back to her office and phoned Ainsley again. She needed someone to confide in. She wanted someone to tell her she was panicking needlessly, that she was distraught, that she was having nightmares and hallucinations.

"I'm sorry," Ainsley's receptionist said, "but as I told you, Dr. Wilson . . ."

At that moment, Marni was swamped by the most intense desire to hold Matthew, to hug him, to sit him on her lap and read him a story. The need overcame logic, caution, fear. "Tell Dr. Wilson," Marni said, "that I have to cancel tomorrow morning's appointment. Can I reschedule for Monday? Thanks."

She called Sergeant Murphy's number again, but he had not returned to his office.

She called Anderson's office and told his secretary she regretted she had to cancel that evening's dinner engagement. She'd get back to him. She considered giving some explanation to Roger, but decided against it. She'd be back in the office the next morning. To her secretary, she said merely: "Got a new listing to look at. I'll be gone for the rest of the afternoon."

She took the subway to Harvard Square. She went into the Harvard Coop, browsed through textbooks, and slipped through the staff doorway, down three flights of stairs and out to the back laneway. From there, she doubled back through the main floor of the Coop to Massachusetts Avenue, crossed the square, and ducked into Holyoke Center where Hertz had an agency. She rented a car for the day. If anyone was keeping tabs on her Pontiac, he could sit and stew in the Exeter Street garage all day.

As she drove out along Trapelo Road and onto Route 2, heading northwest toward the Vermont border, she began to feel foolish. Melodramatic. As though she were playing a silly childhood game of cloaks and daggers. She also checked her rearview mirror constantly.

6: Wilderness, Vermont

At Route 91, halfway across Massachusetts, Marni turned north and drove through pine woods toward the Vermont border. She stopped at Greensboro, still on the Massachusetts side, filled up with gas, and called Eva from a pay phone. There was still no answer. It was four o'clock. Still Thursday, still February 11, still less than twenty-four hours since the first telephone threat had disrupted her sleep. She couldn't believe how much had happened in so short a time.

Nothing to do but keep driving north.

Sergeant Murphy kept driving. He had gone past the gates of his son's school at least ten times now, and he should have been back at his office. It was odd how you could stake out a house full of armed drug dealers with a kind of intensely alert calm, but go weak at the knees when you were summoned to a serious discussion with your kid's teacher.

It had been a hell of a day. Right after he'd left the real-estate office and that young woman—Verstak, wasn't it?—yes, the one who'd made him feel anxious somehow. Why? Because he could smell fear, yes, that was why. That was why he'd had a sudden impulse to hold her. Though it could also have been, he supposed, because he simply wanted a reason to hold a woman again, because he wanted . . . well, best not to go into that. Anyway, it could have been simply that he'd been caught off guard, disoriented, because of that gold-leafed Madonna on the wall behind her—he remembered the jolt and the sharp, unexpected nostalgia he'd felt; he remembered the icon that

that? Whenever he saw her, he felt tenderness and clumsiness in equal parts.)

"I'm sure you will understand," Sister Agatha said crisply from behind her desk, "why I thought it advisable to bring both of you here together." Even Sister Agatha wore street dress. (These days, were there any religious orders that didn't?) Nevertheless, Sister Agatha managed to convey a powerful suggestion of starched wimple and forbidding black habit.

The two parents, estranged, settled themselves guiltily into armchairs. They watched Sister Agatha's neat fingertips keeping some sort of score, bouncing gently and precisely off each other.

Jake cleared his throat. "What exactly has Brian done, Sister?"

"Your son is acting out, Mr. Murphy."

Ah. Jake gritted his teeth. More pop psychology, you got it by the bucketful these days, in the police courts, from talk-show hosts, from schoolteachers, from nuns.

"I understand you are a policeman, Mr. Murphy." Sister Agatha did not bother to wait for confirmation. "Which no doubt accounts for a certain fascination with the more unseemly . . . with, ah, *depravity* on your son's part."

Jake raised his eyebrows and looked at Judy. She was twisting a Kleenex to shreds in her hands and looking fixedly at a spot on Sister Agatha's desk.

"The children of broken homes," Sister Agatha continued, "have a particularly difficult—"

"Do you mind telling me exactly what Brian has done?" Jake asked abruptly.

Sister Agatha pressed her lips together. She spoke of skipped classes and inattention, of poor performance on tests, of an unfortunate incident when Brian had locked himself into a cubicle in the toilets and other boys had heard him sobbing. Jake felt something like a grappling iron turn in his stomach and looked at Judy, who looked fiercely back, full of hurt and anger.

But you were the one who wanted to leave, he reminded mutely. You were the one who said I was impossible.

You *were* impossible, her eyes said. You were never *there*. Out all hours of the night, me never knowing if you would come home in one piece. . . .

I know, I know, a cop's life, it's not fit for. . . .

Not knowing if it was *really* work that kept you out, her eyes accused. Or something else.

There were no other women, you *know* that. I worked like a. . . .

Weren't there? her eyes challenged. Never?

Well, once or twice maybe, meaningless occasions, you can't possibly. . . .

If you cared enough, you'd change, you'd make sure. . . .

And there it was again, the same old impasse, the same old carousel, they'd gone around it a million times, with words, with tears, with silence.

He said stiffly to Sister Agatha: "My wife and I—"

"Former wife," Judy said bitterly.

He looked at her sadly. "My former wife and I have agonized about the effect on our children. We know that nothing. . . ." He moved his hands helplessly. "We're doing the best we can."

"And then," Sister Agatha said, "there is the matter of the drawings, a rather more serious affair, which has occasioned disciplinary action."

Jake looked at Judy, but Judy didn't know about the drawings either.

"What drawings?" he asked, since this was clearly the next line in his script.

Sister Agatha opened the wide drawer in the center of her desk and took out a folder. She opened it and laid it flat on her blotting pad, facing out. She motioned for the guilty parents to come forward. Judy's hand flew to her mouth to cover a small gasp. Jake registered a striking charcoal sketch of a reclining nude woman, her thighs and pubic hair rather prominent, the rest of her foreshortened. Sister Agatha leafed through six sheets of heavy art paper. There were several sketches of breasts . . . well, of women with their arms raised languidly to their hair, their large-nippled curves dominating

"Brian," Jake said gruffly. "Your mother and I. . . . We're not too impressed with your choice in magazines. It's a bit, you know. . . ."

Brian made a grunting, strangled sound as he got out of the car. "I'm sorry I embarrassed you, Mom." The *mom* was emphatic, and Jake felt pointedly excluded. Brian slammed the door and ran up to the house.

"I was going to tell him that I thought the drawings were. . . . I think he has enormous talent," Jake said plaintively.

"You could. You could go in and tell him."

"Yes," he said apprehensively, turning off the engine. "All right."

But they sat there not moving for a while.

"Kathy and Jake Junior," he began. "Do you think they're . . .?"

"They're fine."

"Crying in the toilets. Christ!"

"What about me?" There was a quaver in Judy's voice. She took a deep breath. "It still feels like half of me got ripped away."

He put his hand on hers. "I'm bad news, Judy. Just not much good at living with people. Old habits die hard, I guess."

"You like it, don't you? Living alone."

He shrugged and grimaced. "Yes and no." He couldn't really pretend he was hurting the way she was. "I've got my work."

"Yeah." She shrugged, smiling bravely. "Want to come in for a cup of tea?"

"Sure."

"And you'll speak to Brian?"

"Okay."

Judy smiled. She looked beautiful when she stopped being bitter.

But halfway up the path, they both heard the beeper of the police radio in the car. They both paused. "Better see what it is," he said. "Middle of a case, there was a stabbing this morning, seems to be a shake-up in—"

"Sure," Judy said tightly. "We wouldn't want to interfere with your work."

"It might be nothing," he said, dashing to the car.

"Sure."

"Wait. Wait till I find out what—" But he heard the front door slam before he'd even radioed in that he was receiving. And, damn it, he'd have to leave immediately. Was there any point in going in and trying to explain? Where would that lead? He sighed helplessly: more bitterness, that was where it would lead.

To have loved so incompletely. . . .

He gunned the engine and drove off.

On Route 91, Marni kept driving north. Snow lay deep, then deeper, and the only color was the dark green of the somber regiments of pines. She wound down the window, wanting to breathe in the resin that always had the fresh smell of hope to her, but the rush of icy air numbed her senses, made her gasp.

After Brattleboro, she turned off 91 and followed the winding secondary roads toward Wilderness. Narrow even in summertime, the roads were more like tunnels in winter. The country plows went through once after each snowfall, clearing a width of not much more than a single lane. On either side, snowbanks towered like the waves of an arctic ocean. And then winds and drift kept further nibbling away at the driving space. At times she felt the dangerous slide and sway that happened when a patch of black ice lay underneath a shawl of blown snow. She reduced speed, peering for the hand-painted sign on an oak. There it was: Thrush Farm. And an arrow. She turned into a laneway usually plowed by Steve himself on his farm tractor with a plow attachment in front. The plowed groove was so narrow that the snow flaked away in curls from the door handles on each side and fluttered into the air like doves.

It was nearly five o'clock now, and the thick smoke of a winter twilight fell into every hollow. Just the same, at least three times she was certain she saw the red flash of toboggans or the blue of children's scarves. But when she stopped and opened the window and called out, the splashes of color twisted and vanished like dervishes.

Ahead she could see the floodlight on the farmhouse porch. Neither Steve's nor Eva's car was visible, presumably because both were in the garage, which had been made by converting one end of the stables.

But the old pickup truck, not shoveled out, poked its red cabin roof out of a snowbank. And the snowplow tractor was parked to the side of the stables.

Marni parked beside the tractor. It was only forty-five minutes since she had called. Nevertheless there was something so reassuring about the sight of the lighted farmhouse, so *normal*, that Marni did not for a minute expect to find anything other than the usual scene inside: everyone back from their wood gathering or sledding or whatever it was they had been doing; Steve reading by the fire; Eva cooking over the wood stove; their three children plus Matthew sitting around the big pine table. A farm door is never locked. Marni simply opened the door which led directly into the living room and called.

The light was on and the room was empty.

"Eva?" she called again, walking through to the kitchen.

There was no one there, either, though there were signs of meal preparation in progress. Beside the sink was a cutting board and large paring knife, and a cluster of onions and two green peppers. One of the onions had already been peeled and chopped and placed in a pan on the stove top. A bottle of cooking oil stood in readiness beside the stove, *The Joy of Cooking* was propped open at Gaston Beef Stew. The large pine table was set for dinner with a gingham cloth, flatware, glasses. In the middle was a bowl of holly and pine sprigs.

The quietness of the house was eerie.

Marni flicked on the switch in the center hallway and climbed the stairs to the bedrooms. There were only two rooms upstairs, one on either side of the hallway. Steve and Eva's room was tidy, the bed undisturbed. The children all slept in the long dormer on the other side. The four little cots looked as innocent and untroubled as pictures in a child's storybook. On Matthew's bed, a cluster of small, cuddly toys huddled together on the quilt. Marni bit her lip hard and knelt beside the bed and buried her head in the pillow. She held a teddy bear hard against herself and fancied she could smell the faint sour-sweet smell of her child's body.

Everything's all right, she told herself. Nothing is in disarray. They obviously expect to be back for dinner. Something perfectly ordinary came up. Maybe one of the children had to be taken in to Brattleboro

to the doctor. Kids did that sort of thing all the time: they tumbled off
sleds and twisted ankles, they fell out of trees, they ran high fevers as
sudden and unpredictable as flash floods.

Marni would wait. She would in fact finish cooking dinner for them
while she waited. She went back to the kitchen and opened the fridge.
In a large Corningware bowl, two pounds of good sirloin had already
been thawed and cubed, ready to be added to the stew. She found
celery and carrots, spices, flour for thickening the gravy. Flour. Why
not make muffins or popovers to eat with the stew? Matthew would
love them. (*Mommy made these.*) And Eva too, coming home to a
dinner someone else had prepared.

Not that Eva minded anything, really. Right from their childhood
together in Jamaica Plain, Eva had been the placid one, the one who
took it for granted that she would be happy (wasn't everyone, most of
the time?), the one who dreamed of living on a farm, of picking berries,
of making jams, of lots of children underfoot. Farms ran endless
generations deep in Eva's blood, maybe centuries deep. Her parents
were Hungarian immigrants. Through grade school and high school,
Marni and Eva shared secrets and dreams. When Marni went to
college (the Boston campus of the University of Massachusetts, a state
university being the only affordable option), Eva worked in her uncle's
restaurant in Boston. She made goulashes and rich cream-cheese
pastries and waited on tables. That was where she met Steve, a sixties
dropout with long hair who wanted to go up country, build a log cabin,
farm the land; who wanted a peasant wife, the kind who gave off a
sense of contentment and could bake bread; who wanted Eva of the
deep blue eyes and long hair that hung to her waist.

The day that Marni's father had Geraint Finnbar come to the house
to assess the Ukrainian icon, both Marni and Eva were there. Geraint
flirted urbanely with both of them. Afterwards, Eva said to Marni: "I
don't like him."

"Why?" Marni asked. (She had found him charming, had felt a buzz
of excitement from the way he looked at her.)

"Because of his hands," Eva said. She thought a man with such soft
white hands, such clean, translucent fingernails, was unnatural. When
she met Steve, he had already dropped out of Harvard and was

working on a commune in New Hampshire. He came to the restaurant
on a visit home to his parents, and his fingernails were black with loam.
Marni liked Steve because Eva was in love with him.

Anderson, whom Geraint had brought by for a visit a week later
(he'd made an offer on the icon), could not abide Steve, "that
pony-tailed radical, that rich kid slumming it in the backwoods." He
and Geraint used to trade jokes about Steve—though all of them only
met once, at a ghastly and memorable dinner that Marni's father gave
to celebrate Marni and Anderson's engagement. Yet curiously, the
Steve jokes went on and on, for years. This seemed to have something
to do with the fact that Steve, much younger than Anderson and
Geraint, had gone to a rival prep school. For Anderson and Geraint,
Marni thought, it was like pulling an old stuffed felt ball out of a
childhood toy chest and playing catch with it. A nostalgia habit.
Remember the Righteous Vegetarian with the ponytail? Anderson
might say. St. Steven the Martyr? Geraint would answer. And they'd
be off again.

Marni and Eva delicately avoided discussing their menfolks'
opinions of each other.

Both girls had been married at the age of eighteen. Reluctantly,
Anderson accompanied Marni to her friend's wedding; it was the
second and last time that Anderson and Steve had met. Eva and Steve
moved immediately into the Vermont farm. (It was given to them by
Steve's father, an executive at Xerox, as a wedding present; Steve said
it was the duty of revolutionaries not to look gift horses in the mouth.
"Thanks, Dad," he had said in his wedding speech. "I'll use it as a base
from which to launch a subversive against Xerox's investments in
South Africa and Latin America." The guests had laughed uneasily.
Anderson had reported this speech to Geraint, and the two had made
satirical mincemeat out of it for months.)

About once a month, Marni would drive up to Vermont to visit.
Anderson declined to go with her.

Marni was twenty-two when her marriage was publicly over,
though it took nearly another two years for the annulment to come
through. She discovered she was pregnant as the ecclesiastical and
legal negotiations were proceeding. She panicked. She told no one but

Eva and Steve, who counseled secrecy. For the remainder of her term, she stayed on the farm with Eva, who was pregnant with Deszo, her second. They invited Marni's father up for a visit about six weeks before Matthew was due. "You'll be able to visit the baby here whenever you want, Dad," she'd explained. "But because of the annulment, we have to keep this totally secret for at least a couple of years." She'd seen the pain in his eyes. Three weeks later, he'd had a heart attack. And three weeks after that, the two births occurred within days of each other, at the farmhouse, a local midwife presiding at both. Eva's Deszo and Marni's Matthew were like twins. It was logical and natural that Matthew stay there until the annulment came through. And after that. . . . A farm was such a perfect place for a child to grow up. Until Marni could get herself financially secure, until she could buy her own place in the country, it seemed cruel to Matthew to disrupt his life. And there was the fear that Abigail would somehow legally seize her heir, would obtain custody rights and incarcerate him in the "proper" kind of boarding school, would secure some kind of injunction against Marni as mother.

Sometimes such things seemed improbable to Marni; sometimes not.

She kneaded the popover dough and thought of the way Matthew made angels in the snow with Deszo, their laughter rising like vapor. She saw him almost every weekend. Still, she thought with a pang, it was Eva he instinctively ran to when he fell and hurt himself.

She visualized a room in her Beacon Hill condominium for Matthew. She visualized dropping him off at nursery school in the mornings, having dinner with him in the evenings, taking him to the swan boats on weekends. Yes. Enough of cloak and dagger, enough of fear. She would tell Anderson. To hell with what Geraint thought about the effect this would have on Andy. It seemed quite likely to Marni that Andy would be rather proud of the existence of a son, as long as no child-raising demands were made upon him. What would upset him (and Geraint knew that only too well) would be his extreme anxiety about his mother's reaction. But Marni would see a lawyer and have a document drawn up repudiating all inheritance claims to the Thorpe line and wealth. After all, that was surely all Abigail would care about. And Marni would be the one to broach the lion in her den.

She put the popovers in the oven and stirred the stew. Tasted it. Delicious. She set the timer for the popovers. She checked her watch. To her astonishment, it was nearly seven o'clock.

What could possibly be keeping them in Brattleboro so late?

She pulled on her boots and a parka of Eva's, went out onto the porch and peered beyond the lamp into the darkness, willing a car to appear. Nothing but the silent night pressed up against the ring of light. Acting on sudden impulse, she trudged across the courtyard, pushing against fresh snow, and opened the side door into the garage. Eva's car was there, but not the old station sedan, the one Steve used to take produce to the health-food stores in Springfield and Boston. The Rainbow Chariot, they called it. It had been painted years back, in the psychedelic sixties, marbled with color, a peace sign in Day-Glo orange on each door. Well, Marni said to herself, obviously if they were all going out together, they would need the station sedan, wouldn't they? She walked back to the house, shivering. The woods pressed densely up against the edges of the clearing. A mournful wind disturbed the pines.

Just as she put her foot on the porch steps, she heard the phone ringing inside. Oh, thank God. She raced into the house and grabbed the receiver. "Eva!" she gasped. "Thank God! Where have you been?"

There was a startled sound, a kind of glottal grunt, at the other end. Then a silence. "Hello?" Marni said, unsure of herself.

And a man's voice echoed, "Hello?" as though the two voices were parleying, circling around each other, establishing credentials. It was not Steve's voice.

"Oh," Marni said. "I'm sorry. I thought you were—"

"Steve there?"

"No, I'm sorry. Can I take a message?"

"Take a—? What the fuck? Who the hell are you?"

And before Marni could come up with a dignified and chilly response, he hung up.

Marni paced the living room, boots and all, oblivious to the slush marks of snow she left on the polished wood floors and braided rugs.

She went onto the porch again. The woods were full of ominous sounds. An owl hooted and she jumped. A thousand eyes could have been watching from the darkness, and a frightful smell—

Oh God, the popovers.

She rushed into the kitchen to see smoke spiraling from the oven. When she scraped the charred lumps into the bucket for the compost heap, something like a child's nighttime terror gripped her and she began to shake. She had to sit down. Her hands and face were covered with sweat.

The phone rang again and she leaped at it. She put the receiver against her ear, trembling, and said nothing. The caller also waited, a fearful silence humming between them. She counted ten, twenty, thirty. She was afraid to hang up and afraid not to. Finally she heard a click at the other end.

Now she was desperate to speak to *someone*.

She called Anderson and got no answer. She called Roger and got his machine. She called Ainsley and got the answering service. She dialed three digits of Sergeant Murphy's office number, and then stopped because of the pointlessness of leaving yet another message with some young officer assigned to the night shift. In desperation, she dialed the remote-control code number that allowed her to pick up messages from her own machine. Her own voice, cool and collected, fully in charge of its complicated life, spoke to her. Then came a message from Mrs. Melody Summers in Florida, who would be returning to Boston for a St. Patrick's Day party and would like the tenants out of her place for that week; another tenant left a message to say that the garbage disposal wasn't working; then, out of the blue, came Eva's voice:

"Marni? Me. Listen, I'm calling from a gas station beside the turnpike. I'm on my way into Boston, I'll explain why when I see you. It's just . . . (sigh) . . . it's complicated, it's not good. I'm scared, Marni. Um, I guess I should . . . I've got the kids and Steve with me. See you in . . . oh, God, you'll be thinking it's—No, listen, Matthew's perfectly okay. This has nothing to do with Matthew. It's. . . . "(There was a break in Eva's voice, and something that sounded rather like a sob.) "God, isn't it weird the way things always happen to us together? (Sigh.) Well, I'm near Springfield, so I should be at your place in about two hours, depending on traffic. And on weather. It's snowing again. See you."

Marni hung up and dialed the code again, relistening to Eva's voice, listening to the tones, the silences, the sighs.

Then it came to her that Eva might even now be waiting, locked out of the apartment with the blue floral sheets, watched by someone with a slight, sinister lisp. And why would Eva have left with onions half-chopped on a cutting board? She turned off the element, poured the stew into a casserole dish and stuck it in the fridge.

Just as she was leaving, the phone rang. She stood there, heart pounding, indecisive. Then she picked it up. "Yes?" she said.

She heard breathing, then a click.

She ran across the courtyard and threw herself into her car, then locked all its doors. As she skidded and slid along the barely plowed lane toward the highway, she recited part of Eva's message over and over to herself: *This has nothing to do with Matthew.*

On Route 91 South, after Brattleboro, the driving was easier, though it had started snowing, and scuds of white kept coming at the windshield like wraiths on the attack. Just as they were about to reach through the glass, the wraiths twirled themselves upward and vanished. *Nothing to do with Matthew,* she repeated to herself over and over. Or with the death of Joseph Lucyk? asked some random loose wire in her mind. The car bucked and slewed as though the question terrified it. It was the only car on the road. On either side the woods stretched darkly and unendingly away. They were full of menace. When she saw the lights of Springfield and the turnpike entry ramp ahead, Marni felt as though she had emerged from a voyage through hell.

She collected her turnpike ticket and asked the green-uniformed woman in the booth: "How're the driving conditions?"

"The plows have been through once," the woman said. "But there's blowing snow, and it's very slippery. You're advised to keep under fifty. Been a couple of bad accidents. Coupla deaths, I heard. Jesus, it's freezing."

The woman slid her window shut, and Marni eased the car into the slipstream of the turnpike. The driving wasn't too bad, though occasionally she would feel the slip and slide of the tires on a slick patch of packed snow. She turned on the car radio but could get no music through the static. She would have liked to drown out the beat of the car engine, which kept saying: Joe Lucyk, Joe Lucyk, Joe Lucyk. Or: blue floral sheets, floral sheets, floral sheets. Just after crossing the exit for Route 95, she could see ahead the flashing blue light of a plow, then a cluster of flares and the rotating orange light on the cabin of a tow truck. One of the accidents. They were still clearing it away.

As she got closer, she could see a semitrailer pulled to the side. And then a small, crushed vehicle being hitched to the tow truck. Probably rammed or sideswiped by the semi. She slowed to see how badly the smaller car had been hit, and in the light of the flares she saw the rainbow colors and the luridly orange peace signs.

Oh God, she thought, instinctively jamming on the brakes and thus causing the car to slew violently on the snow-slick road so that she was careening toward the tow truck and the Rainbow Chariot, sideways, sideways. . . .

In the nick of time, her survival instincts took over. She steered in the direction of the slide, pumped the brakes gently, gently, regained control, eased to a stop. She slumped over her wheel, trembling.

The man from the tow truck was opening her door. "Jesus Christ, woman!" he screamed. "Don't you know better than to jam on brakes in the snow? You all right?"

She nodded. "The accident," she said. "That car you're . . . I recognize it. What happened? Did the people . . .?"

She was afraid to finish the question.

"Rammed," the tow-truck driver said. "Semi driver lost control on the snow or something. Rammed the car on the passenger side. Man on that side was killed. The woman was driving. She's critical. Been rushed to Mass General."

Having ascertained that Marni was all right, he strode off to his truck, and she had to rush after him to ask about the children. He was backing the truck up, getting the hook in position, and she had to shout over his engine. "The children?" she called. "What happened to—?"

"What?"

She cupped her hands and shouted again: "The children?"

"Mass General," he shouted back. "Pretty bad, I heard." He idled the engine, getting out to check the hook. "Not family, I hope?"

Marni just kept on nodding and nodding, tears streaming down her cheeks.

"You in shape to drive on?" The man was concerned.

"Yes," she said. "I'll be fine. I've got to get to Mass General."

7: Emergency Ward

Corridors endless and harshly clean, trolleys, nurses, the smell of antiseptic, that awful, intent hush that presses down on the borderlands, the spaces between life and death where the critically injured hover. Marni had had no idea how frequently ambulances arrived at the emergency ward of a big city hospital, how often the hurried whisper of trolley wheels bore bloodied and moaning bodies down polished vinyl passageways to the operating rooms. Sometimes the bodies on the trolleys were completely still and silent, and this was worse.

Marni drank her third cup of burned black coffee and paced the waiting room.

"You can see them now," a nurse said. "They've been sedated. Your little boy has a cracked rib cage, but that's the worst of it."

They were all in the one room, four pale survivors on four narrow metal beds. There was a great blue-purple welt on Matthew's forehead, and the cut on his lower lip made it balloon like a small pontoon, a cartoon mouth. ("His teeth went right through it," the nurse said. "From the impact.") He was thickly bandaged from waist to armpits. But when she bent over him, she could hear the sweet, choppy sound of his breathing.

She put her cheek against his, and the nurse turned tactfully away. "I'll leave you alone," she said gruffly. "Just for five minutes."

Marni blinked. The nurse was handing her a cup of tea, but Marni didn't want tea. She reached convulsively for Matthew's hand and touched a small coffee table. His bed was no longer there.

"You fainted," the nurse said. "Blacked out for a couple of minutes. Happens."

"My son?"

"Perfectly all right. He'll sleep for about ten hours. They'll all be okay in a few weeks. The children, that is."

Something clenched itself tight in Marni's chest. "And Eva?"

"That's the mother?" the nurse asked.

"Yes."

"We still don't know. But we're hopeful."

"I have to see her." Marni tried to stand, and sank weakly back onto the sofa. "Where am I?"

"Emergency ward still. We keep rooms for relatives, especially parents. You can stay the night. It's quite common, this. Shock."

"I have to see Eva."

"Not tonight," the nurse said. "Drink this. It'll help you sleep."

In her dream, Marni climbed the stairs of the house in Jamaica Plain behind Joseph Lucyk. There was an opening about the size of a mailbox slot in Joseph's back, and she could see right through it to the stairs stretching on ahead of them.

"Joseph," she said, curious. "Where did you get that hole?"

"That's the question," he said. "That's the missing piece."

"Missing piece?"

"In the puzzle."

Through the hole she could see the upstairs landing and the attic window. The scream reached her right through the hole. It was through the hole in his body that she saw the kids with the knife, and Matthew, all bloodied, lying in the snow.

She screamed and screamed through the window, but the kids with the knife heard nothing.

"I'm coming, Matthew, I'm coming!" she screamed. But her legs refused to move. Her legs felt like lumps of granite. And when she twisted her body around, when she grabbed hold of the banister to pull her paralyzed limbs downstairs, a great door, thick as the door of a vault, slammed shut in front of her. A man stood on the far side of the door, his hand on the doorknob, pushing it shut.

"Wait!" Marni begged. "Please help me, please let me through."

"Terribly sorry about this," he said politely, smiling. (She could hear the lisp on his *s* sounds.)

"Why are you doing this?" Marni sobbed. "I don't understand what any of this is about."

"It's about Matthew's death," the man said.

Marni screamed and screamed.

"Drink this," a nurse said. "Your son is doing just fine."

Jake Murphy slept badly. He replayed endlessly the conversations he'd had, and the ones he hadn't yet had, with his son.

At about five in the morning, he got up, rubbed the fog off the window, and groaned to see the amount of snow that would have to be shoveled before he could move his car. Snow was still falling. He made coffee and sat in his dark living room looking at the golden puddle of street light.

This was what he knew: things were going haywire. Tremors like the advance shocks of a major earthquake were moving through Boston's drug scene. Somewhere, it seemed, there were powers that sensed change coming: a new president, it wouldn't really matter which, a PR crackdown on drugs expected, things out of kilter, a countertide playing the changes. Known dealers behaving oddly, sons growing up overnight, total strangers arranging deaths in police-staked locales, former wives vacillating unpredictably between warmth and hostility, stabbings, a young woman with a Madonna and Child on her wall frightened of something (a death threat? or a death on her hands? a too convenient stabbing near a property of hers?), extra territorial deals, post-marital temptations, a young woman who looked at him as though she wanted him to . . . no, as though he wanted her to want him to . . . and then immediately after leaving her office, that call about the dealer's car, and it turns out, when he finally gets back to his office and spends half the night in front of a computer screen, it turns out that that car had made an irregular drop last week too, in the street where the stabbing took place, in the street where Ms. Vulnerable Elegance has her property; and it further turns out that another car, which usually does make a drop in that very area, failed to show up on its regular run yesterday—it could be random, waves within chaos, a general panicked grab; or it could be connected by lines as yet untraced. It could be connected by lines as fine and invisible as a woman's hair, by hair in the streetlight, by that gold, the way it puddled at the window, by the gold leaf on the Madonna and that woman's frightened face which begged him to. . . . He fell asleep at last with the coffee mug resting on the arm of the chair, his fingers still on the handle, and was jolted awake at seven in the morning by the phone.

The car that failed to show up for its Jamaica Plain drop route yesterday, the car that should have made a drop in the very street where the stabbing took place, had been involved in a major accident last night. This was unlikely to be a coincidence. There were living passengers at Mass General.

He pulled on clothes, coat, and boots and pushed through the soft foot of snow on his path. Then, fuming, he came back for the shovel on the porch.

A watery light dripped through the hospital blinds. Marni looked blankly at the plain white sheets for a second, then the nightmare came flooding back. (*I don't understand what any of this is about,* she cries to the man behind the door. *It's about Matthew's death,* he says.) Frantic, she got out of bed and ran down the corridor in bare feet. At the end of the passageway, there was a desk and a nurse. Not the same nurse as last night.

"Excuse me!" the nurse said, startled, authoritative. "Excuse me, you can't—"

"My son," Marni said, sprinting by.

The nurse, swift on her crepe-soled feet, followed, caught her arm, restrained her. "You can't—" she began again.

"My son, Matthew Verstak," Marni said. "I have to know—"

"Your son is fine. I'll let you see him if you promise—"

"I promise."

And he was still sleeping peacefully, the swelling gone from the lower lip, the bruise on the forehead a more ghastly purple, the purple of eggplant. The faces of Sasha and Deszo showed similar cuts and marks; little Tina, with two broken legs, sported casts from the waist down, and clear tubing dripped fluid into a vein.

"None of them on the danger list," the nurse said. "They were very lucky. The grandparents are here, arrived about two in the morning, but I'm afraid they . . ."

Grandparents? Steve's parents, Marni thought. She'd met them a handful of times, at the wedding, at the farm.

"They're in shock," the nurse said. "Their only son, apparently. They're sleeping down the passageway. Poor folks."

Marni swallowed. "Eva?" she asked.

"Still critical."

"Will she—?"

"We're hopeful," the nurse said. "That's all I can tell you."

"Can I see her?"

The nurse hesitated.

"She's my oldest friend," Marni said. "Her own parents are dead."

"Just for two minutes," the nurse said.

Eva looked like the Sleeping Beauty, a pale orchid in a jungle of suspended bottles of blood and fluid, stamens of tubing sprouting wondrously from her body. Eva the earth mother, the peasant woman, the woman who left an onion half chopped on a cutting board, whose voice was still on Marni's answering machine.

Why? Marni asked her silently. Why? Why?

"You'll have to leave now," the nurse said. "I suggest you go home—"

"No," Marni said sharply. "I want to be here when my son wakes."

"Of course. Can you remember your way back to the relatives' lounge? There's coffee and—"

"Yes, thank you." Marni paced and drank coffee and paced. She went through the front lobby and did a brisk walking tour of the grounds. She returned to look at the sleeping Matthew, she paced. She considered calling Anderson but was afraid to. She considered calling Ainsley, Dr. Ainsley Wilson, but it was still too early in the morning. She paced through the reception area, down the front steps, another tour of the grounds, back, down the corridor where Eva slept, and there, suddenly, she slammed into Sergeant Murphy. Not that she could remember his name, just that he was the man who promised safety. It was all she could do not to rest her cheek against his tweed shoulder and sob.

"Ms. Verstak!" He seemed startled, then curiously excited. "What are you doing here?"

"It's Matthew," she said. "My—friends of mine." (Could anyone, ultimately, be trusted?) "In an accident."

She was trying to remember what she'd told Sergeant Murphy, how much he knew. Did he know about Eva and Steve? No, she didn't think so. He knew about the house in Jamaica Plain, he knew things from way back, about Joseph, for instance, Joseph's stabbing . . . My God, was that yesterday? Only yesterday? Was that possible? "Sergeant . . .? I'm sorry, I can't seem to. . . . I'm not in great shape, I'm afraid. I can't even remember your name."

"Murphy. Jake Murphy." His eyes were bright, missing nothing. When a police detective slams into a major coincidence, his synapses crackle. "The, ah, the accident that your. . . . By any chance, the one that occurred on the turnpike near Worcester last night?"

"Yes. That's the one."

"I think," he said, "that we should talk."

In the hospital cafeteria, Sergeant Jake Murphy dropped sugar cubes into his coffee.

"If I drink any more," Marni said, "I'll start sweating caffeine."

"The man who was killed." Sergeant Murphy stirred his coffee slowly and watched her. She felt that every twitch and reaction were monitored; she didn't feel quite as safe as she had before. She felt that she was looking at yesterday's Sergeant Murphy through the wrong end of a telescope. "The passenger in the car." He took a notebook from his pocket and flipped it open. "Steven Proctor. What relationship was he to you?"

"None, directly. His wife is my oldest friend."

"I see." He frowned a little, puzzling at something. "And when did you learn about the accident?"

Marni sighed. "That's a long and complicated story. I *saw* the car beside the highway, and the tow truck. It was pure chance." She grimaced. "Well . . . not chance at all in one sense. I'd just been up at the farm in. . . ." (*Is it safe, is it safe to tell him? The hospital knows now, or at least that nurse does, that Matthew's my son. There's no point in . . . but what if Andy or Abigail hears before I've had the legal renunciation drawn up?*)

"In what sense not a coincidence?" Sergeant Murphy asked.

Marni took a deep breath. "One of those children is my son."

Sergeant Murphy blinked and tapped his spoon lightly against his saucer. He stared into his cup as though trying to read the meaning of her words in the surface molecules of coffee. At length he gave up. "I don't quite see the. . . . That was why you saw the car? You were following it?"

"No. Well, yes, in a way, I suppose. I'd gone up to Vermont to. . . . He lives with Steve and Eva, you see. Did." She felt a hollowness inside her. She had never been close to Steve. Perhaps she had been too much influenced by Anderson's view of him. But to Matthew he was Daddy, and a good father, too. Matthew would be devastated. She knew so little, far too little, of her small son's pains and hopes and fears. She'd been so interested in keeping him safe, building a life so she could support him, always planning for some day when it would become magically possible (physically, financially, emotionally) to claim him in public. Maybe she'd invented reasons to put that day off. It was time, it was definitely time to change things. "Uh . . . pardon?"

"I said: We know the car belonged to them," Sergeant Murphy repeated. "Did anyone else ever use it?"

"No one else knew that he was mine," Marni said, following her own maps of thought. "At least, that's what I thought."

"The car," he said. "Can you tell me—?"

Marni leaned across the table and grabbed Sergeant Murphy's wrist. "But now someone is trying to kill him."

The detective's eyes seemed to quiver with intensity, concentrating. "Yes?" he breathed. "Who? Who's trying to kill who?"

"My son. Someone wants to kill my son."

"Why do you say that?"

He was watching her like a hawk. Explanations rose in her throat but got stuck there. He'd promised protection, and what good had it done? "I tried to call you," she said plaintively. "Just after you left, yesterday. I left a message."

"I know," he said. "You'll find a message in your office to say I returned your call."

She pushed her fists into her eyes, concentrated, shook her head. "I can't tell you because it doesn't. . . . No, it just doesn't make sense. And I'm afraid of letting the wrong detail slip out and. . . . I'm afraid for my son."

"I understand," he said quietly. He tapped his spoon against the table, a light rapid drumming sound, a sign that all his senses and thought processes were on red alert. "Suppose I ask some questions, and you just answer the ones you feel you can?"

She nodded.

"All right, then. Let's take this step by step. First the car. Were your friends in the habit of visiting you in Jamaica Plain in that car?"

"Pardon?" It was as though the questions reached her through a fog. She had trouble focusing.

"Visit you. Your friends, Steve and Eva. Did they visit you in Jamaica Plain in that car?"

"Visit me? No. I always went up there. To Vermont. I don't live in Jamaica Plain, I live on—"

"Vermont. That's where the car would be, usually?"

"Yes. A farm in Vermont. Steve grew organic foods."

"Hah!" Interrupted, disoriented, Marni watched him for some signal, some clue as to what they were talking about. Her line of thought had been mislaid. "*Organic*," he said.

"Yes," she said doubtfully. Was that what she'd been talking about?

"He'd built up a small clientele, he took produce to the health-food stores in Springfield and Boston."

"In that car?"

"Well, I think so. Mostly in that one."

"*Organic!*" Sergeant Murphy's exclamation was half amusement, half sarcasm. "Health-food stores. Well, I'll tell you, Ms. Verstak, why *I* come to be here. I had a call from our narcotics squad. That car has been fingered. Been used to distribute crack and coke to the street dealers. It has a regular run, with twelve drop-off points in Jamaica Plain and Roxbury."

"My God!" Marni said, faintly. She heard again the catch in Eva's voice on the tape, the almost sob. *This has nothing to do with Matthew.* She saw Eva's kitchen, the cutting board, the onion. "Something strange," she said. "The chopped onion just left. . . . That's not like Eva." And with nervous urgency: "There's a tape I should play for you. It's on my answering machine. Eva must have made the call about twenty minutes before the accident."

"If it *was* an accident," he said.

"Actually, you can listen to it from that pay phone. I'll give you my remote access code."

He patted her arm gruffly and smiled, and he seemed again the bringer of comfort who'd sat in her office the day before.

"What do you think it means?" she asked him after he'd listened to the tape.

"I'd say someone was putting pressure on her husband. He knew too much, perhaps. Or someone thought he did. I'd like to dub a copy of that tape. Can you take me to your apartment?"

"Now? I want to be here when Matthew wakes."

"Yes, of course." He was sympathetic, gentle. "Whenever you're going home will be fine. I'll check back here late this afternoon. Around five."

The day passed as dreams pass. Sometimes Marni was at Matthew's bedside, sometimes pacing, sometimes making phone calls to her office (she left a message for Roger, saying that a friend was critically ill in the hospital) or to Ainsley's office (could she possibly see Dr. Wilson some time today?). Every hour, she asked for a report on Eva's condition (no change, no change). She watched Eva's forest of tubing move ever so slightly as she breathed.

Matthew drifted in and out of consciousness. Once he raised heavy eyelids and looked at her and said drowsily: "Hi, Mommy. We're going to Boston."

"Matthew," she said, holding his little hands against her cheeks. But he drifted back into a place of medicated limbo somewhere between sleep and waking. Sometimes the other children surfaced from their haze and she talked soothingly to them. Where's Mommy? they asked. Where's Daddy? But she stroked their foreheads and said simply: "Your grandpa and grandma are here."

Sometimes she talked to Steve's parents, who came and went and came again, and looked haggard. Once Steve's mother broke down while she and Marni were alone in the lounge reserved for relatives. "I never understood it," she sobbed. "He shut us out. I never understood what we did wrong." She looked at Marni with eyes wide with a kind of horror. "Do you know, if Eva hadn't brought the children down to Boston twice a year without telling him, we would never have even seen our own grandchildren."

Marni thought of Anderson and his mother. Parents and children, she thought, have a million ways to hurt each other. And what would Matthew grow up to think and say of his sometimes mother, the absentee? Something that felt like a tapeworm of pain coiled and twisted inside her body, sending out messages of grief. She watched her skin dully, waiting for bruises to form. She put her hand on Steve's mother's arm. There was nothing to be said.

"I think you should go home and sleep," said a nurse, peering in. "The children'll sleep most of the day. We're not anticipating any change in Mrs. Proctor's condition."

"Yes," Marni said. "All right." She dialed her office again and thus picked up the message from Dr. Ainsley Wilson's office. Dr. Wilson had had a cancellation, and could see Ms. Verstak at four o'clock today, if she was interested.

Today? Marni thought, confused. What day is today?

"That message came in about an hour ago," the office secretary said, as though reading her thoughts. "Would you like me to call and say you'll be—"

"Well, but I don't . . ." Marni couldn't quite get a grip on time. Her digital watch said 3:37 p.m., a cryptic message. "What day is it?"

"It's Friday," the secretary said. "February 12th. Are you okay, Marni? Your voice sounds kind of funny."

"Yes. Yes, I'm fine," Marni said. "Call Dr. Wilson's office and let them know I'm on my way."

8: The Analyst

"One of the problems," Dr. Ainsley Wilson said, "is the distortion of ego boundaries." Dr. Wilson was not a rigidly orthodox analyst, though she had been trained as one. Radical articles and feminist critiques, and certain circumstances of her own life, had had a bearing on her practice. She did not require her patients to lie on a couch, but faced them. She preferred dialogue to the patient's monologue. She gave suggestions. "Disturbed people put themselves at the center of the universe," she said, "but also at its edges. They think that everything that happens does so with direct reference to them."

Marni's eyes were wide with surprise. "You think I'm a disturbed person?"

"Isn't that why you are here?"

"Well, yes, right now I'm disturbed. But that's because of external events. I get a threatening phone call in the middle of the night. My foreman is stabbed to death about an hour after I've been talking to him. I get another phone call from someone who knows about my foreman's death, and who threatens my son again. Then my son is almost killed in a highway accident. Naturally I'm disturbed. I'm terrified."

"Of course you are," Dr. Wilson said quietly. "And with good reason. You have harbored an intense fear about your son's safety for a long time, and now that fear has become concrete. Your son is in the hospital. You are in shock." Dr. Wilson's voice was soothing, the voice of compassionate sanity. "But, as you now know, your son is not in critical condition, and he is under expert care. It is important that you do not work yourself up into an irrational spiral of anxiety. I want you

81

to relax your arms, your shoulders, your neck . . . I want you to breathe deeply, slowly. . . .

"Good. Now, calmly, I want you to think about things. There has been a highway accident during a snowstorm. There was a stabbing in Jamaica Plain. These are horrible events, but they are not uncommon. In fact, in this city, we must sadly acknowledge that both events can happen almost any day of the year. Does it seem likely to you that these events were planned with special and malevolent intent toward you?"

Marni was too bewildered to be angry. "Are you telling me that this is all pure chance? That nothing is. . . . What about the phone calls?"

"Tell me," Dr. Wilson said quietly, "what is your worst fear in relation to your son?"

"My worst fear? Well . . ." Marni closed her eyes and saw Vermont, the times when she had watched Matthew running through the apple orchard and playing with Sasha and Deszo and had thought: if harm should come to him, I couldn't bear it, I wouldn't be able to go on living. She remembered how anxiety had hit so suddenly that it felt like cramps in the stomach; how she had had nightmares in which Abigail Thorpe appeared as a witch who did terrible things to children. "My worst fears aren't rational," she said, embarrassed. "I've had nightmares about what Abigail might do to him, but of course I know that's crazy. It's just a reflection of a pervasive fear that he'll come to harm."

"Exactly. And our fears, if we don't bring them out into the open and acknowledge them, can be powerfully disruptive forces. They can take on a life of their own."

"What are you saying?" Marni demanded.

"What do *you* think I'm saying?"

"I think . . . I think you know that I don't feel certain I really got that phone call. I'm afraid I dreamed it." She buried her face in her hands. "Or maybe I want to convince myself I dreamed it, because that's less scary than if I really got it."

"Go inside yourself," Ainsley said quietly. "Examine your fear. Which is greater? Your fear that you did or your fear that you didn't get the phone call?"

"Phone *calls*," Marni said suddenly. "Because he called me again, I forgot to tell you. The man with the lisp did. It was the same man who called me at my office, right after Joseph Lucyk had been stabbed."

"That call would have gone through a secretary?"

"Yes," Marni frowned, thinking back. "Well, usually. With that particular call, I just picked up and answered myself. Because I'd been talking to the police and I thought it was going to be more—"

"So there's no external evidence that there *was* a call?"

Marni could feel fear and bewilderment rising in equal parts. "Is it possible I could have imagined a daytime call too? Am I going crazy?"

"It is astonishing," Ainsley said soothingly, "the tricks the frightened mind can get up to. But being frightened is not the same as being crazy. I simply want you to consider the possibility that your guilt and fear about your son, which you keep repressing, are taking on a life of their own."

"Wait a minute." Marni pressed her fingers against her forehead. She was picking her way through a mine field. It was important to walk slowly and notice details or her life might blow up in her face. "I don't think I've repressed my fear. I'm very conscious I'm afraid. Right from the moment that I realized Andy was gay—"

"You were afraid of your husband because he was gay?"

"No, not of that. I adored him, I still do. But there were things. . . . It was impossible, it was hell living with Andy. I was just a child, really, eighteen, but younger in lots of ways. When you grow up in a Ukrainian home, well, I was very protected, a total innocent. I didn't know anything. And yet I knew something was wrong, the way he. . . . Sex, you know, was like a chore, like he was gritting his teeth, and he could hardly wait to get into the shower afterwards." She sighed. "And yet we're so fond of each other, we really care about each other. It was a relief to him when I realized, and we could talk about it. He'd felt guilty from the start, he said, taking advantage of my ignorance. I was eighteen, and he was thirty-five. He did it to please his mother. He was afraid she'd find out he was gay. He was under enormous pressure to marry and produce an heir. He was afraid of her, he's still afraid of her.

He's forty-five years old and he's terrified of his mother. Can you believe that?"

"Oh yes," Dr. Wilson said. "It's not so uncommon."

"The only reason she agreed to an annulment was because it didn't look as though I was capable of producing the heir. I knew if she found out I was pregnant, I'd be shackled to Andy for life, so I've always been anxious about her. I haven't *repressed* it in the least."

"You were afraid you wouldn't get out of the marriage. But you did. And yet you continue to conceal the fact of a child. And he's how old now?"

"Five."

"Five years of anxiety so great that you cannot let anyone know you have a child. What exactly is the worst of your ongoing fear?"

"Well, I . . . It's not rational, I know that. Keeping Matthew a secret, I mean." Marni sighed and massaged her forehead with her fingers. "But it's not totally irrational, either. I suppose I'm influenced by Andy's fear of his mother. Even though I've always known he must be exaggerating." She looked at Ainsley and looked away. "Well, part of me knows that. The other part is sure she'd do *something* if she found out. Something unpleasant. I just don't know what. That's. . . . It's just a general fear of harm coming to him, I guess."

"Whereas the fear is almost certainly unwarranted. As the rational part of you knows." She waited for Marni to look at her. "Suppose you were to go to this woman directly and tell her? She might be delighted to have an heir after all. Or she may be furious and cut your son out of the inheritance. Or she—"

"I don't care in the least about that. I'm going to have a legal statement drawn up, renouncing all inheritance rights. I'm going to tell Andy and let the chips fall where they will."

Dr. Wilson smiled. "I'm pleased to hear this. You are facing your fear head on and taking responsibility for your own life. I predict that once you have done so, these manifestations of your anxiety disorder will peter out."

"Gosh," Marni said, feeling as though she had been handed sun and moon on a platter. She looked out the window at a clear sky. She felt weightless, she felt. . . . A small cloud scudded across the space behind the casements. "But what if I *did* get those phone calls?"

"Then the fact of your son's being under close observation and expert care in a hospital would be reassuring, wouldn't it?"

"Well, for the moment, yes," Marni said uncertainly. "But let's just hypothesize that there *is* someone making death threats about Matthew, and that's why he's lying injured. And there are all these details of my life that someone knows."

"And your rational mind tells you it's impossible for any one person to know these details?"

"Yes, it does. But—"

"That is what strikes me, you see. The mind responds in funny ways to repression. All these years you've hidden Matthew, you've put a ball and chain on your life, on your tongue, on your identity as a mother. For all practical purposes, you've had to block Matthew out."

"No," Marni protested. "That's not true. Almost every weekend, I went—and Eva and I talked about the situation a lot."

"Ah. Eva." Dr. Wilson gave the word a certain significant emphasis.

Marni bridled. "What do you mean?"

"You have very complicated feelings about Eva."

"What? I do *not*, I'm quite simply and uncomplicatedly grateful she's been a mother to. . . . She's my closest friend, she might be dying, for God's sake."

"Why do you think you feel so defensive?" Dr. Wilson asked.

"I'm feeling like a rat in a trap," Marni said. "I mean, I come to you for support, and I feel as though I'm taking a test and no matter what answer I give, it's going to be the wrong one. In the past twenty-four hours, there've been two deaths, threatening phone calls, my son has had . . . and here you're. . . ." She gripped the arms of her chair, tried to calm herself. "I'm sorry," she said. "You've been so helpful in the past that I. . . . When everything suddenly went haywire, I instinctively wanted to turn to you. . . . But there's something terribly strange going on. There's even something strange about the way you're . . . as though you're part of this weird nightmare I'm having. You seem different. I know that's ridiculous." She buried her face in her hands. "Maybe I *am* going crazy, that's what you're telling me, isn't it?"

"Going crazy is not a very useful term," Dr. Wilson said quietly. "I'm simply asking you to consider the possibility that your repressed anxiety has formed a kind of subterranean torrent in your psyche and is suddenly erupting into—"

"But Eva's in critical condition at Mass General," Marni protested. "She might die, for God's sake. That's *real!*"

"Yes, and it is very frightening," Dr. Wilson said. "It's like a match to the powder keg of a great many other fears. And of guilts, because you are grateful to Eva, you are heavily indebted, but you are also jealous of her role in your son's life, and you feel guilty about your jealousy."

"It's true," Marni sighed.

"But do you really believe—" Dr. Wilson was leaning forward, speaking very gently "—that the night, the snowstorm, the truck driver, and I don't know how many other variables, all conspired in sabotage against you personally? That the road conditions were personally vindictive? That in fact there are no boundaries between your ego and the world out there?"

"Well. . . ." Marni faltered. "No, of course not, but I. . . . Surely even you must find the coincidence of Joseph's stabbing and the accident. . . . Isn't it just as difficult to see those as—"

"No," Dr. Wilson said. "As we've already acknowledged, statistically both of those events happen with frequency in this city. I say this not to diminish the real tragedy of those two events, but to prevent you from further torturing yourself with phantasms."

Marni rubbed her forehead. Then she said: "Well, if you're right . . . then I don't have anything to worry about. If it's all in my mind, then Matthew's perfectly safe, right? And that's all that matters to me. I can stop hiding him. I can tell Andy and his mother. . . ."

"That is what I strongly recommend." Dr. Wilson smiled.

Marni felt as though lead weights had been lifted from her chest. She felt flooded with warmth and informality. "Ainsley, you're so . . . so *quick.* You always manage to zero in on what's bothering me."

It was as though Ainsley, with a few swift strokes, could cut away the brush, all the stuff that was irrelevant, as though she already knew what was really the trouble before she was told.

"It's downright spooky," Marni said, "the way you can. . . . It's a gift, I suppose. I've thought that right from the beginning. It was so amazing, the way you just approached me at that party and we talked, and next thing—it was as though you knew I was desperate to talk to someone, and next thing I knew, you were offering to be my therapist."

"That's not quite the way I remember it," Ainsley smiled. "I believe that you asked if I'd consider seeing you."

"Did I?" Marni laughed, and shielded her face with her arms in mock self-defence. "Okay, okay, you win." Far be it from Marni, who apparently could not even distinguish between a phone call and a dream, to challenge Ainsley's version of events. Anyway, however their association got started, it had been beneficial. "I feel so much more tranquil now. I can't wait to have this all out in the open and—" A thought struck her, the image of Eva amidst her tubes, then Sergeant Murphy's face over his coffee cup. A persistent little dart of anxiety suddenly slipped in again, winging right by Dr. Wilson's calm assessments. "The police," Marni said, frowning. "The detectives. *They* don't think Joseph's stabbing was routine, they think there's something very fishy about it. And now that I . . . Some stuff is just coming back to me. Sergeant Murphy doesn't think the crash was an accident."

"Ah, the police," Dr. Wilson said dryly. "I really can't be responsible for a detective's febrile imagination. He'll have to go to his own analyst." She smiled, inviting Marni to share the joke.

"You don't take them seriously? You don't think they—"

"I'm sure lurid fantasies would be an occupational hazard. I'm sure they have a need, amounting to an obsession, to impose a theory and order and meaning on the random violence they see all the time."

"That's . . . I've never thought of that." It seemed to Marni that her little raft of reason was riddled with leaks. "I suppose you're right. It's just that. . . ." She was casting about for something at the tip of her mind. What was it? Too much had happened, and she could not concentrate. What was it? Oh, of course, Steve's car. "I remember what I wanted to say." She felt suddenly triumphant. She felt, somehow, that Ainsley would be pushed to explain the phone calls. "There's hard evidence of a link between Joseph's stabbing and the crash. Steve's car has been used for drug trafficking in Jamaica Plain."

Dr. Wilson raised her eyebrows. It was gratifying to startle her. She turned away and looked out her window for several seconds. Then she said slowly: "An analyst is not always right, of course. We make what I suppose you could call informed and intuitive guesses. We base them on observing certain patterns of behavior over and over again."

"So you agree that the evidence on the car—"

"I'm not agreeing or disagreeing. I'm sure, from a police point of view, there may be a link of sorts between a car crash and the drug traffic; and another link between the stabbing and the drug traffic. But are they one and the same link? And from the point of view of your emotional well-being, which is the issue concerning us here, is it your rational assessment that either of these links could have anything to do with you personally?"

"Well, no. It's crazy. It couldn't have. And yet—"

"The habit of pathological anxiety is hard to shed," Dr. Wilson said. "We call it 'awfulizing.' Always expecting the worst. You can actually make the worst happen that way. You have to break the pattern, you have to take the dramatic interventional action."

"Like what?"

"That has to be your decision, though I've already indicated the direction that—"

"You mean telling Andy and Abigail?"

"Are you going to do that?"

"Yes, I am. I'll call Andy tonight. I'm hoping to see him for dinner tomorrow night."

"That's good," Dr. Wilson said. "That's excellent. We'll talk again after you have done so. And now your hour is up."

"I feel a million times better than when I came here. I'm so glad you staked me out at that party."

Ainsley raised her eyebrows. "You should ask yourself why you find it necessary to disclaim responsibility for your actions so constantly, Marni. We'll work on that too. Next time."

Outside, Marni noticed that the air itself had become easier to breathe, more tranquil. She took the subway to Charles Street. How simple, how foolish, anxieties could be, she thought. How lucky she was to have met Ainsley.

But as she walked along the pedestrian overpass across Storrow Drive, as she faced the massive brick hulk of Mass General, as she watched one ambulance after another screaming into the emergency area, she seemed to re-enter the fog of old fears. Perhaps it was the vision in her mind's eye of Eva, still sprouting tubes, still fighting for her life. Perhaps it was the consciousness that a fractional change in timing, road conditions, alertness of truck driver, weights of vehicles, any micro-difference might have meant that Matthew would be lying alongside Steve in the morgue. With every step, her uneasiness grew, and a feeling—she could not put her finger on it—that there was something about the session with Ainsley itself that was bothering her. She replayed the session in her mind. She concluded that it was simply her long-ingrained habit of anxiety resisting the prescribed cure. She was *awfulizing* again.

Yes, surely that was it.

She crossed Charles Street and entered the massive lobby of Massachusetts General Hospital. The feeling of unease increased with every step. When she collided with Sergeant Murphy, she felt panic, then confusion. Why was he . . .?

"You promised me a copy of the tape," he said.

"Tape? Oh. Eva's phone call." She put her forehead in her hands, massaging her temples. "I'm sorry, I can't seem to keep track of anything. Can you wait till I've seen Matthew?"

"I'll be waiting out front in my car," he said. "The dark blue Chrysler."

9: Jake

He dubbed Eva's voice from Marni's answering machine onto his own tape, then stood uncertainly in her living room.

"Would you like a drink?" she asked.

"Well, ah . . . sure." He watched the way her hair fell across her face as she opened the fridge.

"Beer? White wine?" She was looking back over her shoulder. "Or Scotch? It's in that little cabinet beside the sofa."

"Beer," he said, and then felt somehow clumsy as he watched her make a white wine spritzer for herself.

The beer surprised her. There were all sorts of things that didn't match; the tweeds and corduroys and pipe went together, but they didn't match the detective part; the beer matched the Special Drug Task Force part, but didn't quite seem to go with his knowledge of Ukrainian icons. And that way he had of greeting and taking leave, with his hands; the way he'd given his arm when she got out of his car, there was something curious about it, but she couldn't put her finger on what it was.

She sat on the sofa, kicked off her shoes, and curled her feet up under her. "What a day!" she said. "I can't believe how much has happened in the past forty-eight hours. Less than forty-eight hours."

"Now you can relax."

"Yes." She looked around her apartment: the signed lithograph on the wall, the smooth curves of a soapstone carving, the potted plants, the window that looked out on the glittering lights of a winter's night in Boston, down Beacon Hill, toward Cambridge. There was a dark ribbon winding its way between the lights: the Charles River. She usually felt deeply tranquil sitting on that sofa, looking out at that view. She should be able to relax. Matthew was out of danger, safe in a hospital bed, less than a mile away. She should be able to dispel the malaise that had settled on her as she was walking toward the hospital. It had not lifted since.

She looked out at the city glitter and the dark loops of river. There were other black lines, the grid of the fire escape that went by her window. The landing was level with her sill. In summer, when the apartment became impossibly hot and steamy, she would put a piece of plywood over the iron rungs of that tiny landing (it was three feet square), and balance a chair on it, and sit out on the makeshift balcony, queen of the Hill. The uphill view, crowned by the golden dome of the State House, was hidden from sight, but looking down she could see the Charles Street Meeting House where Sojourner Truth had once pounded the pulpit, the lights of Fenway Park, the spires of the Harvard houses. She was on the fourth floor. She could follow the twists and turns of the iron stairs all the way down to Acorn Street, the cobbled lane at the back of her building.

A couple of times over the year since she'd bought the condominium, she'd thought idly: If anyone wanted to break into a fourth floor apartment. . . .

"Two nights ago," she said, shivering, "I thought I heard someone on the fire escape." She waved a hand, mocking herself. "It was just the tree tapping against the window. Took me ages to work up the courage to look. Silly, huh? A bit paranoid, right after the phone calls."

"What phone calls?" Sergeant Murphy was wondering again what it might be like to take this woman in his arms and offer comfort. Sometimes this happened to a police detective. One thing led to another, and sometimes . . . but it was usually a fleeting thing. Protect me but don't touch, was the usual unspoken message that women gave out.

She had put one fist to her mouth as though installing a blockade against stray words. She hadn't intended to mention the phone calls, he could see that. Her hair fell across her face and the light caught it.

What would happen, he wondered, if he leaned across and touched it? Or lifted it aside so that he could see her eyes? But he took another mouthful of beer and said only: "Have you been getting threatening phone calls?"

She sighed and looked up at him then, through her lashes and the curtain of golden hair. "I suppose I should tell you. I suppose I have to tell you. I mean, it's evidence, more or less. Or it could be. It seems to be another link, besides Steve's car, between Jamaica Plain and the accident." She sighed again. "That is, if there really was a phone call that night." Her malaise had risen from a hum to a drumming bass chorus, but she could not *name* it. There was something . . . something . . . it was like trying to recall a dream that has slithered just beyond the reach of consciousness, but hangs on in the wings of the mind like a tantalizing mist.

"Sergeant Murphy, let me ask you something first. Do you think—"

"Jake."

"Pardon?"

"Call me Jake."

"Oh. Um, Jake. Thank you," she said, a little awkwardly. "Mine's Marni. Um, Jake, do you think—Earlier you seemed to be suggesting. . . ." She put her wineglass on the table and walked restlessly into the kitchen, stood there vaguely, walked back to the sofa again. She laughed. It was a small, nervous, self-deprecating sound. "Maybe I'm reading things into what you . . . but you seemed to suggest there's a link between the stabbing and the car crash."

"Maybe not a direct one. But some sort of link. That's my hunch."

"Hunch." She said the word slowly, tasting it, sucking it, to see what kind of meaning it held. (*Ah, the police.* Ainsley's well-bred cynicism floated between them, a faint echo. *Occupational obsession . . . the need to impose a theory . . . obsessive need . . . obsession for order. . . .*) "And do you ever find . . .? Are your hunches . . .? Are you ever wildly wrong?"

He took a long, deep draught of beer. "Well, actually no." Their eyes met, held. "I get these powerful reactions from down here somewhere." He patted his stomach just below his belt. "And my gut seems to know what it smells."

He liked this. He liked sitting in the elegant living room of a beautiful woman, talking to her. Just talking. Two *thinking* people. It was as though he'd slipped back into his former life, except that of course in that former life, talking to a woman in this way was quite impossible. He liked the way she looked at him gravely out of her gray-blue eyes, waiting for his answer, interested in it. Too many people had this image of cops as apes who played with guns and billy clubs, or pulled stiffs out of rivers, or hung around with street sleaze looking for tip-offs and protection money. He'd become so used to the image that he'd moved inside it, he wore it nearly all the time, like a costume—though the costume didn't fit very well, he supposed. People were always telling him he didn't look like a cop, didn't sound like a cop. But it always turned out, because of the costume, that they expected him to behave like one, all quick instincts and no intellect.

But cops *thought*. Not just himself (who'd been required to do little *other* than think in that prior life), but other cops too. All cops. They thought a lot. They thought all the time, as a matter of fact. If you hoped to survive in the inner-city beat, you had to be a thinking man. And not just about who was doing what. He himself puzzled a great deal about how and why his hunches came so early on, when he scarcely had two bits of evidence to rub together, and why they always led in the right direction. He'd never figured out an answer, but he never got tired of poking at the question, analyzing backward, running the mental movie of the case in reverse after it was all over. "This feeling just comes out of nowhere. Not always right away. I have to sort of go inside all the details, every tiny detail counts for something, I have to go inside them and wait. It's like a . . . a bit like a skyrocket going off inside my head. Once that happens, it's a matter of tracking down the evidence to match the gut feeling."

She was nodding. It matched something she knew about herself. He liked this. Usually, these days, he could only talk like this to some lonely drunk in a bar late at night; not because the drunk was interested, but because he'd just sit there with his glazed eyes, listening. Gave you a chance to talk about it out loud and listen to yourself. Marni Verstak kept squeezing her eyes shut and running her hand through her hair, combing it with her fingers, as though there was something—a hunch, perhaps?—lost back there.

She asked: "When did your hunch come about Joseph Lucyk?"

"Instantly. Sometimes that happens, but I don't know why. It can take me weeks to figure out *why* I smelled what I smelled. I got a call from McCarthy before they moved the body, that's our policy now. And the second I looked at the body, I knew something was wrong. So when these other details started coming in, from the woman with the baby, you know, about the fancy car and the white driver, and the kids on the block who didn't recognize the muggers, and so on, I didn't feel surprised. I already knew."

"How?"

Jake frowned. "I still don't know how. I'll have to think." He put his beer on the coffee table and began to pace about her room. He stopped and looked out the window. He seemed to be talking to himself. "Something to do with the way he was lying. . . . The snow, the blood." He made one circuit of kitchen and living room. "No, not the blood. Something about. . . ." He seemed to be muttering his way through a mental checklist. She heard, indistinctly: "Head . . . eyes . . . wound . . . throat . . . wound, no . . . legs, arms . . . his arm. Yes, his arm." He turned suddenly. "That's it. His arm was broken. But not from his fall. It was not the arm he fell on. And your other worker, the one watching from the window, he heard the scream, saw the kids slash the old man's throat, then he started to run downstairs. So they cut his throat and *then* they broke his arm. That's not the way kids—if they're high, it's just rage, panic, run. There's something . . . it's different, like vindictive, or a message . . . that was it."

"Yes," she said nodding. It was as though she too had gut feelings and directions and momentums, but hadn't yet uncovered the map she'd been using. "But the link with the accident?"

"The report on that car came in from the narcotics squad. Then I bump into you at the hospital while I'm checking it out. Sirens went off." Strictly speaking, technically speaking, he was out of his mind talking to her like this. This kind of loose talk could cost your life. But the place just below his belt said he could tell her anything, and his arms said they should be holding her.

Her eyes were wide. "You thought I was involved?"

"Connected. Involved in that sense. Not—" Then he remembered that there'd been a split second of vertigo, the fear that her hands were not clean. It had vanished when she'd raised her startled eyes to his, in the hospital corridor. As she was doing now. That same look. "Not in any criminal sense."

She smiled mournfully. "Well. That's something, at least."

"Tell me about the threatening telephone calls," he said.

She pressed her fingertips against her eyebrows, massaging. "Ainsley thinks they might be messages from my unconscious. My worst fears welling up." She ran her fingers up across her forehead, through her hair. "Which is plausible, but I don't know, I don't know." There was a long pause. "And she says that your hunches . . . that the police . . . that you do the same kind of thing."

"Imagine things?"

"Yes. And then make them happen somehow."

"That's what you think?"

"That's what Ainsley thinks. I just don't know."

"And who exactly is Ainsley?"

"Ainsley Wilson. Dr. Wilson. She's my . . . analyst, I suppose you'd say. Psychotherapist."

He grunted, a sound composed in equal parts of surprise and contempt.

"You don't think much of—?"

"Shysters." He couldn't keep it back, that little explosion of anger. "Sorry. But if you'd heard as much contradictory evidence in court as I have. Pick a number, pick a psychiatrist. You can produce one to say any damn thing you want. Both sides do it all the time. Might as well pull a horoscope out of a hat."

Marni laughed. It was refreshing to hear someone say that out loud. She went to the fridge, took out another beer, poured it carefully into his glass as though she was absolutely aware that another drink had been at the edges of his thought. He watched the careful way she tipped the glass, pouring slowly, monitoring the foam. He studied the little creases in her knuckles, and the pale pink of her fingernails. No polish, perfectly natural, but shining, somehow. That was the right word for her. Shining. "To tell you the truth," she said, "that was always my view, too. I've had psychiatrists and therapists as real-estate clients, six or seven of them. Every last one of them the most mixed-up, the sickest, the most obnoxious people I knew. Figured I'd rather trust my well-being to a witch doctor."

"Definitely safer," he said, and they both laughed. There was this second when they just went on looking at each other while the laughter died, and he knew she felt it too. One second, maybe two: a little current of electricity zapping between them.

But then she turned away. Not rudely. No, it was graceful. But still—

Big abyss between a woman like her and a street cop. No sense pretending. He'd been born and grown up a street kid, Somerville, wrong side of the tracks; then there'd been that strange interlude, another life for which he sometimes pined; no, that wasn't true; it was just that there were some aspects of it for which he felt a wistful nostalgia, the tranquility, the books, the discussions. But it had never taken. Never had a chance of taking. A street kid was what he was, raised rough, and now he was back on the streets where he belonged. No bridges, either, across that kind of gap. Not often, anyway.

"But Ainsley's different," she said. "One day she just stepped out of the blue, and I'd have to admit—" She'd taken another can of soda and the bottle of white wine from the fridge, and now she stopped in the kitchen doorway with both in her hands. She was somewhere else, seeing something else. He knew better than to interrupt.

"That's funny." She said it aloud, but not to him.

She was back at the cocktail party on Marlborough Street, home of a socialite client of Roger's, Roger fishing for more big business, Marni (on Roger's pep-talk instructions) required to be angling for business contacts too. She remembered how she felt: dreadful. As though she had slammed into a concrete wall. Five nights earlier, euphoric, she had walked along the Charles in the moonlight with Michael Lavan, sat with him in the dusk of Casablanca in Harvard Square, sipping brandy and listening to jazz and considering telling him about

Matthew. He had spent the night in her apartment—here—sitting just where Sergeant Murphy was sitting while she'd fixed him a drink and she'd thought: Will I tell him about Matthew now? And then: Why rush into complications? Why not simply enjoy this, no tangles? She'd tell him about Matthew and Andy and all that in a week or so.

Then, the next day, his wife had called. Chaos. That abrasive, hysterical, ugly call and its nasty aftertaste; Michael's reaction (*as long as we're careful, the world's our oyster*); Marni's response; his reaction to that: the sudden hard look in his eyes. And then the second call from his wife. *He says he's tried and tried to make you leave him alone . . . but you just keep throwing yourself. . . .*

Nasty, but sad, too. His wife's in worse shape than I am, Marni knew; but it gave little comfort.

Marni got through several days at the office like a zombie, reciting various catechisms to herself: *I'm lucky it's over.* But the emotions are slow learners. There were times when she remembered only the feeling of his body and still hungered for it. There were times when she had trouble believing in his Mr. Hyde self. (Maybe she dreamed the bad parts? the calls from the wife?) She had a sense of cobwebs clinging to her limbs, webs of depression. At the cocktail party on Marlborough Street, just five days later, she was still operating on automatic pilot. She would rather have been anywhere else. She was feeling rotten.

And then . . .

Slow motion. She is exchanging chitchat with a woman on the board of the Boston Symphony. Roger is raising his eyebrows with pleasure, signaling: *Go for it, Marni, a fish on the line.* She nods back, she is turning toward the bartender, her eye snags on two women at the other side of the room. They are watching her, discussing her, they see they are observed and one turns sharply away. The other stares boldly back, smiles, and comes toward Marni.

"I was just asking someone to point you out," she says. "I wanted to meet you. How do you do, I'm Ainsley Wilson. Dr. Ainsley Wilson."

Marni feels slightly puzzled, the enthusiasm seems . . . what? a shade overdone. (Yes, that's it. *Click.* Overdone.) Ainsley Wilson's hand is cool to the touch, firm in its handshake. This is business, it says.

But then, curiously, the handshake lingers a couple of seconds too long. Uncertain? Nervous? Ainsley is an attractive woman, dark-haired, elegantly dressed. One corner of her mouth twitches slightly, repetitively, a tic. There is something poignant, Marni thinks, about a flaw in a polished finish. She feels instinctively protective. She is also curious. "Who were you asking? I'm afraid I didn't recognize the woman you were. . . ."

There's a split second when the self-assured face seems to fold in on itself—Ainsley bites her lip, blinks a little rapidly—then the calm is reassembled. Like trick photography. Marni wonders, fleetingly, if she imagined the bitten lip. "Oh," Dr. Wilson shrugs, looking vaguely around. "I don't really know who it was. Everyone seems to know you. You come highly recommended. I'm told you're the one who can find me the perfect office suite in the Back Bay."

"I'll do my best," Marni says.

Then everything goes blank—for seconds? minutes?—because Michael Lavan is in the doorway, just arrived and late as usual. Of course, Michael was expected. Roger requires his team to rub shoulders with the Back Bay social set, which is the real-estate set. Marni has been, she realizes now, looking for an excuse to leave before Michael arrived. When she sees him, the first thing that comes back in full force is their last breakfast, the languid, erotic mood, the way he reached for her and begged: Don't go. But I'm just going to make more coffee, she said. Yes, she has been half hoping she imagined everything since the breakfast. She wills Michael to look at her. He does. His look is expressionless. He looks away as though she were a total stranger.

Well then, she thinks with finality, her nerve ends pinching with something that is apparently pain. Well then. Love comes, love goes. Big deal. That's the past now, and good riddance.

"Is something the matter?" Ainsley says.

"What?" Marni hears Greek or Swahili or the babble of some foreign language. There's a general unintelligible hubbub and this sensation of confused sadness. "What?" she says vaguely.

"It helps to talk. You should talk to someone you can trust." Marni sees a hand on her arm, a bitten lip: vulnerable tics. She wants to trust this voice. "Believe me, you really need to talk these things out," Ainsley says. "Here's my card. Why don't you come and talk to me tomorrow morning?"

From the kitchen doorway, Marni walked out of her trance toward the sofa, smiling. Chalk one up for my sense of reality, she thought. She leaned over the coffee table and poured herself another spritzer, mixing liquids. Mechanically, she pushed a bowl of pretzels toward Sergeant Jake, even said something inconsequential. But her thoughts were still on Marlborough Street tracks.

Two women talking about me . . . Ainsley biting her lip, blinking. *You really need . . . Here's my card . . . tomorrow morning.*

Click, click, click. Ainsley's memory is faulty, she can be wrong. And my perceptions are as reliable as the next person's.

Marni said slowly: "I *did* get those phone calls. The nighttime ones, and the daytime one. The caller has a very slight lisp."

"Tell me everything," Jake said. "Start at the beginning."

"No," he said, hours later. "It doesn't make sense. Not yet. But we have to go inside the details, wait for the patterns to show up. Your caller with the lisp, for example—"

"It's not really a lisp at all, it's just a kind of windiness on the *s* sounds."

"And this Geraint who's very interested in what you tell your former husband. This Geraint is present when you get the phone call from Jamaica Plain, and he already knows you had a house on that street."

"Yes, but that's Geraint. He's always like that, he gets some sort of power from knowing trivia."

"Odd, though," Jake said.

"Yes." Marni was musing on other coincidences. Odd. Two women, both looking at her, one turning sharply away. "It *was* odd, the way Ainsley appeared the very moment. . . . But see, that's what disturbed people do. They take every tiny coincidence personally. Ainsley's right about that, I do think I overreact when I'm nervous."

"Who doesn't?" he shrugged. (You need to charge people one hundred dollars an hour to tell them that?)

She reached for his glass, her glass, and placed them six inches apart on the coffee table. "It's like there are two circles," she said. "Your glass is Anderson and Abigail and Geraint and Eva and Steve, all the people who might have had anything to do with my phone calls, with Matthew. And my wineglass is people I don't even know, drug traffickers, street kids in Jamaica Plain. And the circles don't really have anything to do with each other, except it turns out Steve belongs in both of them."

"Hmmm."

"Now," she said, her hand on the beer glass. "This is the circle I was afraid of. Mainly Abigail. But it turns out that this other one was the circle causing trouble. And since City Council has backed out of my Jamaica Plain project, and I'm stymied, and Steve's dead, the danger's over. Right? I don't need to worry about Abigail at all, even though there might have been things going on in that circle."

"It's always possible," Jake said, "that both circles had their sights on Matthew, and it's pure chance that both were operating at the same time. Maybe they somehow got tangled together. Or it's also possible they're *not* tangled together, that it just happens they have an intersection point and neither knows it. I've had that happen before."

Marni put her hands over her face. "Then I can't even know if I'm out of danger or not?"

"It's always wise to act as though you're not."

"How do we ever know *anything*?" Marni groaned.

"Eventually we know some things for certain," he said. "But I'm never quite sure we know the way we know. For example—" he put his hand on the wineglass "—I've had times when I've gone inside one circle, and had hunches, and tracked them down, and everything falls into place. But it turns out that everything that mattered was going on in this other circle all the time—" he put his hand on the beer glass "—but I got to the right answer just the same. It was a fluke. I used the wrong map, but I got there."

"So you're saying it *could* be Abigail I should be worrying about. And the deaths of Joe Lucyk and Steve—they're just coincidences."

"It's possible. I don't rule anything out. Though my hunch is still that it's more simple. I'm willing to lay even money that in the end it all comes down to crack. It's a multimillion-dollar industry in Jamaica Plain alone. Stands to reason there's someone doesn't want you messing with the market. Someone doesn't want a neighborhood turned around."

"Well," she sighed. "It's worked. I'm at a dead end in Jamaica Plain." She was refilling the pretzel dish. They both seemed to be munching compulsively. They'd both forgotten they had not eaten dinner. "I just realized what I said. Dead end. Not very funny, is it?"

"You might like to know," he said, "that I've got a man at the hospital keeping watch. Just in case."

The smile she gave him was dazzling. "I didn't quite have the nerve to ask . . . in case you thought. . . ." She crossed the room, threw her arms around him, a quick hug. "I'm so glad you've done it." She was gone again, over to the window. He could feel where her arm had touched the back of his neck. Her perfume still hung near his shoulder, a little fog of spicy weather. Or tropical flowers maybe? He didn't know how to describe it.

"You know," she said, looking out at the fire escape, "that first night, I'd worked it out that it had to be some drifter friend of Steve's and had something to do with drugs. I was in *that* circle." She pointed to his beer glass. "The keep-Matthew-a-secret circle. But I guess I was right all along, just like you said. It's just that the drifter belongs in *this* circle, the drug-traffic circle, and I was a few hundred degrees off about how serious." She crunched a pretzel. "God, these things make me thirsty. We need iced water." She went to the kitchen again, restless. "What I can't figure is why Steve would have got himself mixed up with. . . . I mean, he liked to call himself a revolutionary but it was just silly, really. He was a country bumpkin at heart."

"Probably grew marijuana on the back lot and got out of his depth," Jake said. "Wouldn't be the first time we've run into sixties dropouts who landed themselves in that kind of mess. Start out harmless, running grass to flower children, wind up dead."

"Eva knew the pattern on my sheets," Marni said suddenly. "So that would explain—"

"And what about Dr. Wilson?"

Her eyebrows went up, startled. "Oh, she has nothing to do with either circle. Well . . ." She poured iced water for both of them. "It *is* curious. . . . But see, I'm doing it again, making my ego boundaries stretch to the edge of the world, the *disturbed person* syndrome. That's how Ainsley puts it." She raked her fingers through her hair. "Ainsley's okay. But it's just. . . . I think it must be analyst's vanity, you know, the conviction that I approached her." She laughed, picked up a pretzel, looked at it, put it back in the dish. "Ainsley was a godsend, anyway. It's just. . . . Oh, I'm so confused, I don't want to think about anything any more."

He was contrite. "You should sleep. I should've left ages ago."

"Oh no. I've really enjoyed . . ."

"Will you be all right?"

"Heavens, yes." She paused and looked at the window where the fire escape was. "Actually, I'll be a nervous wreck, but I know that's stupid."

He said carefully: "I could, um. . . . If you wanted, I could stay." He cleared his throat. "Sleep on your sofa."

"Oh!" Her sigh of relief was so deep, her smile so warm, that it was all he could do not to touch her. "Could you? Would you?"

"Probably sleep better than if I go off and worry—"

"I'll bring you a quilt," she said.

He did something curious when he said good night. He touched her forehead with his fingers for a moment, the way a priest might. She lay awake thinking about it.

He lay awake too, listening for her breathing in the other room. If he lived in a place like this, he'd have to eat differently. Buy fresh produce from Haymarket, stuff like that. You couldn't bring cardboard cartons of Chinese into this kind of place. Not with those paintings on the walls. If he lived with someone like this, maybe they'd cook together, the way couples did in glossy magazines. He'd be opening a bottle of red wine and she'd be—

He looked up, and she was standing in the doorway.

"I can't sleep," she said. "Besides, I'm starving. Did you eat dinner?"

"No." God, he *was* starving.

"Me either. No wonder we're hungry, it's 1:00 a.m. I'll fix us some pasta," she said. "I've got olives. D'you like broccoli? Sun-dried tomatoes?"

He was not going to admit he'd never tasted sun-dried tomatoes. Life was astonishing, it daily took him by surprise. You started out staring at some poor shit leaking blood from his throat and ended up on Beacon Hill with sun-dried tomatoes and a woman wearing practically nothing. The light over the sink came at him right through that silky nightgown thing, and he swallowed and looked away, concentrating on sun-dried tomatoes. They looked more like red leather than tomatoes, if you wanted to know the truth. But he didn't want to put a foot wrong, spoil things.

"You're not married," she said. A statement.

"Was. Divorced three years back."

"Ah." It didn't seem to be the answer she was expecting.

"Being married to a policeman . . . it must be . . ." She handed him a collander with the drained dried tomatoes, and a knife. He felt a moment's panic. He hadn't the faintest idea what was expected of him. "Strips," she said, demonstrating. "Like this. It must be rough on the marriage. Your wife would be scared all the time."

"Yeah. Well. That's what she said." Not that that began to explain the half of it.

She said, concentrating on the onion she was slicing: "Do you have any children?"

"Three. Brian's thirteen, Kathy's ten, Jake Junior's five."

"Matthew's age," she said.

He made a noncommittal sound. She went on dicing the onion with delicate concentration. She was scraping it into the pan when the phone rang, and she dropped the cutting board. There was a horrible clatter of board and knife against floor, and the phone shrilling on and on, a sound that pierced and shocked like a switchblade knife at the throat.

"What'll I do?" she whispered.

"Answer it," he said. "I want to hear."

He picked up the receiver and held it between them. He nodded to her.

"Hello," she said, as steadily and neutrally as she could manage.

"I'm so sorry about the Rainbow Chariot," the voice said pleasantly, and the slight breathiness on the *s* sounds was apparent. "That was an accident, of course. Wrong person."

There was a wait. Jake shook his head slightly and put a finger on her lips. Marni said nothing, though her heart thumped so loudly she thought surely the caller must hear it.

"I do hope I'm not frightening you. You're not *disturbed*, are you?" the voice asked.

Marni said nothing.

"Here's a thought for the wee hours, then." There was a hint of waspishness to the voice now, a clear note of irritation. "I just wouldn't want you to think that you're out of the woods."

Then the click.

"I can't stop shaking," Marni said.

She held her trembling hands together in front of her face like a child at prayer, and he closed his own around them. "It's all right," he murmured. "It'll be all right." She could feel the rough surface of his palms, a callus on the trigger finger as he brushed her cheek with one hand. She leaned her forehead against his shoulder.

"We've learned something," he said slowly. One of his hands hovered, tentative, then stroked her hair. "We know something we didn't know before. We know whoever it is isn't watching the apartment. He doesn't know I'm here."

She raised her head, suddenly drawing energy from the thought, straightening up. "Or he wouldn't have spoken?"

"Not to a police officer. Not knowingly."

"And something else," she said. "The Rainbow Chariot. That proves he's one of Steve's drifters. No one else would know what he called the car."

"Detail by detail," Jake said. "We close the net."

"Did you get the feeling," she began, "that he was . . . I think he was angry that I didn't panic or plead or something."

"Definitely," Jake said. "He's beginning to blow his cool."

"I'm glad you put a man on duty at the hospital," she said. She was looking at the way he folded her hands inside his. "Jake," she said, "before you were a policeman ... did you ...? were you ever ...?"

It seemed too silly to put into words. She laughed it off. "There's just something about your gestures that reminds me of our old family priest, Father Simeon. It's probably because—"

Jake grimaced. "I trained for the priesthood," he said. "To please my mother." He grinned wryly. "You'd make a good detective, Marni." He ran his fingers through his hair. "Amazing how hard it is to erase that training. But it would never have worked. I dropped out of seminary the week I was to be ordained and broke my mother's heart." He smiled wryly. "Six years in a seminary, you get used to a solitary life. It's not a good recipe for marriage."

10: Big Turk and the Wall Street of Crack

Jake spent Saturday in Jamaica Plain, burying himself in details. And trying to bury his anger. He was angry with that jerk Gatton in the Drug Enforcement Administration.

"The homicide itself, the *body*, is still your case. That goes without saying," Gatton said. "But the wider implications are ours. Federal, that is. Not city or state. It's simply a matter of not duplicating man-hours."

"So why'd you bother sending me the information on that car in the first place?" Jake demanded.

"Inadvertent, actually," Gatton said. (Christ. The way these DEA blowhards talked. Like they had a mouthful of cotton candy. Election year going to their goddamn heads, politicians in both parties giving 'em enough money and green lights to make your head spin.) "Some kid from the First Lady's Campaign Against Drugs brigade, a keener, a flag-waver, more idealism than brains, you know what I mean? They send them over for free," Gatton said, grimacing. Cop to cop: what can you do with politicians? "Traffic division feeds in a highway accident, and the car comes up on this kid's computer. The kid pushes a few buttons, and a street comes up twice: once as a drop point for the car; once for your homicide. The kid puts two and two together and calls the wrong person. Still." Gatton gestured expansively. "We'll give what help we can, naturally. But your Special Drug Task Force is political window dressing, you understand. Public relations. It'd be counterproductive to go meddling in our established lines of investigation, though. The stabbing itself is your ball game, no question. The highway death belongs to Turnpike Authority.

106

Any linkage is ours. For us, it's the wider picture. Putting all the ball games together."

"The World Series," Jake said dryly.

"Exactly," Gatton said, not getting it. Pompous jerk.

"Yeah, well," Jake said. "Thanks." Almost biting his tongue to keep from swinging at the asshole. "What could help in nailing the kids that did it, the stabbing in my particular Little League game, I mean . . ." (Flatter the bastard, since he wouldn't recognize irony if he stubbed his fat toe on it. Let him think you're stuck on the small potatoes. And don't tell him about the white driver who watched while the kids gave it to Joseph Lucyk, no damn way.) "What could help is that rainbow car's route. The other drop-off points. I'd really appreciate it."

He got what he wanted. In a diner under the elevated subway tracks in Jamaica Plain, he passed this on, verbally, to Big Turk, his man on the streets.

Big Turk stirred his coffee with one finger and bit into his doughnut. "Man," he said. "What you messing with, sarge? You guys just playing games, *you* know that. Some very well-connected people putting crack back in the sandboxes just as fast as you take it out. Ve-ry well connected, know what I mean? And all these people got a finger in election pie, got an eye on the future."

"Yeah? Which people?"

"And then there's other people with campaign coffers to fill, very hungry, turn a blind eye if the money's coming in, know what I mean? You got a very big can of worms here."

"Yeah," Jake said. He emptied a Coke can into a paper cup of ice. "You got names?"

"And you also got a lotta very well-connected people not gonna put their silver foot in their mouth."

"Who?" Jake leaned forward. "Do you know who?"

"Maybe. Maybe not. Don't have to know who. Don't have to have brains to figure out it ain't Mickey Mouse waving his wand. We're talking *clout*, man."

"You know this car? Old flower-child car? Owner called it the Rainbow Chariot?"

"Owner's nobody, man. Chicken shit. Some chichi white dude gets his feet wet, thinks he can draw a line, keep his hands clean. Didn't like the heat, he should've stayed outta the kitchen."

"You know he's dead?"

"Yeah, news gets around."

"You know who arranged the accident?"

"Maybe."

"You gonna tell me?" Jake asked.

Big Turk drank his coffee and pulled another doughnut out of the waxed-paper bag on the table and ate it as though he had not heard. Below the table, Jake took his wallet from his pocket, took out a fifty-dollar bill, put it inside a paper napkin, and slid the napkin across the table.

"Jesus, man," Big Turk said irritably, pushing it back. "You don't need me for that, you got the goddamn highway report already. And what the hell good's that gonna do anyone? Fingering some poor sod of a truck driver's got a wife and kids to support, missing mortgage payments on his rig. Sucker gets told to arrange a blowout, he does what he's told." In a sudden excess of rage, Big Turk closed his hand around Jake's empty Coke can and squeezed. The can crumpled like candy-wrapper foil. "Not the kinda crunch you ever get caught in, is it? Paycheck coming regular every month." He took another doughnut from the waxed-paper bag on the table and ate it in two bites. "Trucker's nobody, man. Nobody. Motherfuckers up in glass towers, motherfuckers in their Back Bay condos, motherfuckers all over gonna laugh all the way to their Swiss bank accounts if some trucker gets nailed." He took the crumpled Coke can in his hand, gave a slight twist, and tore it in two. "An accident, man. A blowout. Leave it be."

After a longish silence, Jake asked: "He have helpers, the Rainbow Chariot man? People who made the rounds with him?"

"Sometimes. White riffraff, dropouts, we're talking rich kids slumming in *Ver*-mont, playin' cloak'n'dagger, playin' dan-ger-*ous*." Big Turk turned up the whites of his eyes expressively. "Been stoned since 1960, don't know their ass from a hole in the ground."

"I'm looking for one who talks like this." Jake mimicked the British tones, the slight lisp: *I hope you're not disturbed.*

"Hey, man," Big Turk laughed. "They gonna mail you an Oscar, you don't watch out. They gonna want you on *Miami Vice.*"

"You heard anyone sounds like that?"

"Not me, man. I'll ask around." Big Turk watched the sidewalk beyond the diner. "We all done?"

"Not quite. I also want—"

"Ain't got all year. Not good for my social life, hanging out with cops."

"The stabbing on Thursday, up by Franklin Park. Guy working on this house that's being fixed up."

"Stay away from that," Big Turk said shortly. "You know what's good for you."

"Someone doesn't like the house?"

"You kidding me? Mess around with the marketplace?" He laughed. "That's the Wall Street of Crack, man. That's a dead-end street." He laughed at the unintentional pun. "Hey. A dead-end street." He laughed again.

"The kids who did it, they weren't local. We got witnesses. White man drove the car. You know who?"

"Man," Big Turk said, looking at Jake in disbelief. "You hear me? You deaf or something? You wanna find yourself out on your ass, no pension?" He leaned close across the table. "You know what I'm saying, man?"

"What are you saying?"

"I'm saying, you think the DEA don't know what side its bread is buttered? I'm saying, you think it's pure charisma keeps Noriega propped up? I'm saying, find your man for that rap, you in a whole lot more trouble than if the front page the *Globe* and *Herald* both, got a picture of you with your tail between your legs. You want my advice?"

Jake grunted into his Coke.

"Me, man," Big Turk said. "In your shoes what I'd do is I'd leak a headline. Buy some ferrety reporter a drink and act depressed. POLICE HELPLESS, COP CONFESSES. MORALE LOW. NO HOPE FOR INNER CITY. Send the right message to the right places, know what I mean? Buy some protection."

"There's a lawyer for the company that fixed up the house, dropped some heavy hints about real-estate people, developers."

"Every bagman's dream, man. Every dude selling powder on the street is gonna turn developer, turn respectable, own a glass tower or a shopping mall."

"Company called Olde Pilgrim Realty?"

"Up to here." Big Turk tapped the underside of his chin with the back of his hand. "Still chicken shit, though. Front men. Little people. You not gonna see the ones pulling their strings. And you don't wanna find out."

"You find anything on Mr. Lisp, let me know," Jake said. "Okay?"

"Man," Big Turk said, shaking his head. "You make me nervous."

He took a last doughnut, pushed back his chair and left.

Jake left the diner and found his car intact, a small miracle. Not even a hubcap gone. He had an address, one of the kids who'd volunteered information on the stabbing of Joseph Lucyk. He swung up along the border of Franklin Park, looking for the street the kid lived on. Half an hour later, he had the kid in the precinct office in Jamaica Plain, looking at picture books. Hundreds of mug shots. The kid's name was Leon.

"I don't know," Leon was saying. "I don't know. Like, when it starts, we all looking at the car and the white dude. What *he* doin' here? We smokin' up in this wreck at the edge of the park. Easy and high. So my brain is, like, floating. Then the car . . . shit, man, sudden like a hit is on, car turns sharp in front of us, nose up to the park gates, next thing backin' up into the street. Screaming *re*-verse, like they know it's a dead end, they can't turn round. And we go, Hey, who those kids? They on *our* turf, man. Who those shitheads think they are? Stuff like that.

"But we slow, see. We thinkin' slow and easy. We gettin' outta that car, real slow, like we walkin' in a dream.

"Street has a hump, and they go over the other side, down the dip. We can't see nothin'. We shamblin' down the street, 'Who those motherfuckers think they are, workin' *our* turf?'

"Then, holy shit, that car comes screaming back up and we

scramblin' to save our asses. But I never see those motherfuckers up close, except the white dude."

"Okay," Jake sighed. He had another set of mug shots, not black kids this time. Already on Friday, he'd called a secretary at Olde Pilgrim, posed as a buyer, got a list of brokers and reps. He'd sent the names and addresses of all the males across to Vehicle Registration. Got black and white Xeroxes of their driver's license photographs. Not great, but they would have to do. Enough to give an idea.

"Any of these the man who drove the car?" he asked Leon.

Leon looked and shook his head. "No sir."

Jake gave him a twenty-dollar bill. "You hear anything, see anything, remember anything, you call this number, there's more. Okay?"

"Yessir," Leon said, rolling up the twenty and the piece of paper with the telephone number on it, and tucking both down the instep side of his sneaker.

Saturday afternoon, late, Jake dropped by the hospital, hoping to see Marni. The nurse said she'd just gone home, exhausted. He went back to his apartment and waited an hour and then called to see if she was all right.

She didn't ask if he'd like to come over.

Well, what did he expect?

Maybe he waited a second too long, wanting her to fill the silence. He didn't want to push things, scare her. "If anything happens," he said, "you have the emergency number?" Polite, businesslike, just doing his job.

"Yes," she said. "Thank you."

"I checked in on little Matthew," he said. "I've got a man on duty all night, watching."

"I don't know how to say thank you," she said. The way her voice sounded when he held her after the threatening phone call. (Last night. That was just last night. Less than twenty-four hours ago. How come he felt as though he'd known her for about five years?)

"If it was up to me," he said rashly, "if they gave me the men, I'd have someone watch your apartment all night."

"Jake," she said. He could hear the smile. There was silence for several beats. If she asked, he would be in a cab and over there before she could get the sun-dried tomatoes out of the fridge. "I'll be all right," she said lightly. "By the way, I'm meeting Anderson tomorrow evening for dinner. And I've had a lawyer do a rush job for me. Legal renunciation of inheritance, it's called. Just in case we're inside that circle."

Jake thought: So I won't see her tomorrow night either.

11: Dinner with Anderson

Marni put the long legal envelope on her side plate and looked at her watch again. It was Sunday evening in Harvard Square, and the single man at the next restaurant table watched Marni watching her watch. She thought irritably: If Andy's any later, that man is going to make a pass. She fiddled with the watch at her wrist, worried. If you'd been married to a man for four years, there were certain things you could always tell from his voice. And when she'd called Anderson late Saturday morning, he'd been nervous. There was no getting away from the fact that he had not been at all keen to meet her for dinner.

"Andy," she'd said. "I don't like to sound melodramatic, but I *have* to see you. It could be a matter of life and death."

"I was afraid of that," he said.

And she felt as though she'd been given an injection of ice. The words—the quiet, lusterless way he'd said them—sent panic in all directions at once, to the top of her head, the tips of her fingers, her feet. Even her gums hurt. It *is* Abigail, she thought. And Andy knows something's going on.

She had already arranged to see a lawyer Monday (not Michael, needless to say; she'd called someone in family law, someone who'd bought a condo from her last year). After talking to Andy, she'd had to call him back, sweet-talk him, call in courtesy chips; she simply had to see him on the weekend, before she met her ex-husband for dinner.

"I can't possibly meet you today," Anderson had said.

"Tomorrow then?"

113

"All right," Anderson had said. "Tomorrow evening. Sunday supper. But, ah, I'd rather not meet you at Rebecca's. It's, ah, could we avoid the city? How about Harvard Square?"

"Fine by me. Harvest House?"

"No, that's too . . . I'd prefer somewhere more off the . . . you know, I'd rather not bump into Back Bay people."

His mother. He's terrified Abigail will be there, she thought. With one of her gentleman widowers. All terribly proper. Not a breath of impropriety ever came near Abigail, but her social calendar was almost frantically busy. Was there any cultural institution of which she was not a member of the board? Boston Symphony, the Gardner Museum, Heritage Boston, the Museum of Fine Arts, the Back Bay and Beacon Hill Horticultural Society, Friends of Harvard, Friends of Eliot House, Friends of Lowell House, Friends of Radcliffe, et cetera, ad infinitum. But except for Harvard/Radcliffe receptions, Abigail stayed on the stuffy side of the Charles. She didn't go slumming in Harvard Square.

"Okay," Marni said. "There's a place just off the Square on Winthrop Street. Casa Mexico, it's near Lowell House. Students love it, but you can be sure Back Bay wouldn't touch it."

"Not too noisy, I hope? Something quiet and secluded, so we can talk. And dimly lit."

"Romantic, you mean?" she asked dryly.

He said reproachfully: "That's not like you, Marni. It doesn't suit you, snideness."

"Sorry." He gets all the snideness he needs from Geraint, she thought. She felt incredibly, overwhelmingly tired. "Casa Mexico is exactly what you want. Candlelight and seclusion. It's very popular with homesick Californian and Texan students, but I've never known it to be full. It's in a basement, actually. They've added adobe and piñatas and Aztec suns."

What a weekend.

Waiting in Casa Mexico, Marni kept tapping the legal envelope (its bulk comforted her) and looking at her watch and avoiding making eye contact with the man at the next table. She sipped a frosted margarita. A bright blue piñata dangled above her table, and she watched it twist slowly in the currents from the radiators. Above her head, a basement window in the rough, whitewashed wall looked onto the sidewalk. She studied passing ankles and boots: pull-on vinyl boots with fleece linings from Sears and Zayres (graceless things, but warm and cheap and therefore favored by students); leather and rubber duck-shooters' boots, catalogue-ordered, affluently casual; high-heeled suede calf huggers; the occasional soggy and snow-filled pair of sneakers. Anderson's ankles would be snugly and expensively caressed in kid leather. His boots would have, perhaps, little gold buckles on the side; they would be the kind of footwear worn by a hunting gentleman on his country estate. She watched for Anderson's ankles in the snow above her head. When they came down the stairs to the restaurant, they would pause and recoil a little. This was not Anderson's usual kind of place. Anderson preferred the four- and five-star restaurants where he'd taken her when she was a dazzled eighteen-year-old who worshipped him.

Well, that happens to all of us, she thought. We all find ourselves in places we never expected to be in.

Who would have thought she'd spend a couple of hours a day in an intensive-care ward, watching her son breathe through tubes, his skin translucent? The doctors had discovered a tiny puncture hole in one lung, where the cracked ribs had grazed it. They'd have to keep him in longer than they'd thought. She had sat and stroked Matthew's hair while he slept.

She had stood and watched Eva, hooked up to her battery of machines and monitors. Eva's life was so many graphs on a clutch of screens. There was no change in her condition. The doctors said only: it is still too early to say whether. . . .

And who would have thought that Marni would spend a night with a policeman in her apartment? A cop who'd almost been a priest. A smile played about her lips. It was interesting to talk to a man like that, a man with calluses on his hands and dirt under his fingernails; a man who said vehemently, "Those drug pushers, those shits!" (the things you *expected* a police officer to say), and then, minutes later, talked about the nature of hunches and said: "The heart has its reasons, which are quite unknown to the head." When she'd looked at him with surprise—because somehow it wasn't the sort of thing you expected a policeman to say—he'd added, self-consciously: "Pascal. Can't get out of the habit of reading the *Pensées* at night. One of those seminary things."

When she'd put her head against his shoulder, she'd felt the welt below his armpit, under his coat. His gun. It was a startling, comforting sensation. Interesting. A policeman, a divorced man with three kids, was not her kind of man, of course. But still, he was nice. And intelligent. (Well, of course, if he'd trained as a priest.) And sensitive, too. Gentle. She stroked her own hair, remembering something.

And then to wake up, yesterday morning, and find the same man bending over her, offering a mug of coffee. That was a first. No one had ever done that for her. When she was married to Anderson, the housekeeper used to bring the tray to their room. And those business trips with Michael, she'd been the one who got up, called room service for breakfast, waited on him.

God, what a track record. She'd been in love twice in her life. Anderson and Michael Lavan. It was certainly enough to cure you of such nonsense forever. Forget love. She'd settle for safety, her son's life, turning a neighborhood around. Hah. Scratch that last one. That piece of hubris had cost two lives already. She'd settle for a standard career in real estate, and her son across the kitchen table every morning.

She wondered if Jake Murphy's wife had left him, or he'd left her. And why. And what would his kids be like? It must be dreadful, living with a cop. Just one long crisis. Never knowing when he'd be home again. Or if. Not that the question concerned her. But it had been nice, very nice indeed, to have Jake Murphy call her Saturday evening to remind her he had a man watching the hospital ward. If it was up to him, he said, he'd have one watching her place, too, but they didn't give him enough men for that. Was she all right? Yes, she said. He was on duty, he said. If anything happened, she had the police emergency number? Yes, she said.

It was nice that he called.

Marni looked at her watch again. It wasn't like Anderson to be late. He was so precise about everything he did. She remembered the way he'd had to line all his shoes up in the closet, and how upset he'd be if she (or the housekeeper) bumped one out of alignment. She'd never seen a man with so many shoes. She never knew any human being in the world had so many shoes. (Her father had two pairs, one for work, one for best.) But everything Anderson owned was beautiful. And expensive. And spotlessly clean. He loathed soiled things. They terrified him. When he and Marni made love (a weekly drill, performed religiously on Sunday nights) he would be under the shower within seconds of their uncoupling. She'd listen to the water shussing, shussing, lying there puzzled and miserable, wondering what she was doing wrong. She'd try to—

Beneath the swaying blue piñata, a waiter in a pin-tucked shirt and black bow tie was asking: "Excuse me, are you Ms. Verstak?"

"Yes," she said, her heart lurching. "I am." What now?

"There's a phone call for you. You'll have to take it at the receptionist's desk."

Marni took the receiver and turned her back to the waiter, huddling her arms and shoulders around the phone. "Yes?" she said.

To her enormous relief it was Anderson's voice. "Marni? I'm terribly sorry. I've been delayed."

"What's wrong with your voice? Have you got a cold or something?"

"What? It's hard to hear you. Listen, can I ask a favor? Do you mind coming here? I'll have J.J. Bildner's deliver a gourmet meal."

Marni winced. "I don't know, Andy." It wasn't a house where she felt at ease. She'd known a great deal of confusion and unhappiness as a young wife in that house.

"I really *can't* meet you there, Marni. I'll explain when you get here. And we do need to talk. Just get in a cab."

"Well, okay. See you in fifteen minutes or so."

It was more than ten months since she'd seen him—not since their "wedding anniversary" last April—and she supposed almost anything could have happened in that length of time.

Abigail Thorpe lived at the Public Garden end of Marlborough Street, where the Back Bay meets Beacon Hill. She could walk to the Ritz for lunch in any weather. This was the fashionable end of the Back Bay—though at a tea party early in her marriage, Marni had heard a Beacon Hill matron say archly: Those of us who live on the Hill, Abigail, cannot help looking down on you, can we? And Abigail, quick as a wink, had replied: The Back Bay *knows* who's keeping the Hill propped up, my dear.

Coming off Storrow Drive in her taxi, Marni could look through a gap between buildings and see the cornices of Abigail's house. Her taxi turned right into Beacon and headed west, back toward Massachusetts Avenue, Boston University, and Cambridge. ("I really don't understand why you can't buy a place closer to the Common," Abigail used to admonish her son. But while Anderson couldn't quite bring himself to leave the Back Bay altogether, he did live on its farthest rim from his mother. There were a good eight long blocks of the most expensive real estate in Boston between them. In Boston, this meant he was practically in another country. His mother would shake her head fondly at tea parties. "He thinks he's hiding his wild lifestyle from his mother. He's such a *playboy*. I don't think he'll *ever* settle down. As for grandchildren, I simply *despair*." Depending on what restaurants they frequented, Anderson and his mother might not see each other for months and months at a time—as long as Anderson forfeited opening nights at galleries and the symphony. Or he could arrive late, a debutante on his arm, wave to his mother from his box, and leave early.)

On Beacon Street, in the block between Hereford and Massachusetts Avenue, Marni's taxi pulled up in front of a four-story red-brick building with curved bow windows facing the street. The house was narrow, just the width of a room and hallway, and Anderson (and his art collection) occupied all levels.

Marni banged the great brass knocker, and a male housekeeper answered. He was new to Marni, not someone who'd been part of the household when she'd lived there. He did not seem to approve of female visitors. He did not speak, but took Marni's coat and hung it on the branched Victorian mahogany "tree." He watched while she pulled off her knee-high boots and changed into the shoes she carried with her. He propped her boots beside the massive old snuffling radiator to dry out. He took the drawstring shoe-bag and slung it over a peg below her coat. Then he nodded toward the dining room to indicate Marni was expected.

The dining room was dimly lit, all the candle sconces on the paneled walls burning. Andy stood with his back to her, in the deep niche of the window seat that looked out onto the backs of other buildings. Here and there, between those buildings, one could catch glimpses of Storrow Drive and the frozen Charles.

As soon as he turned, even in the murky candlelight, Marni understood.

"Oh Andy," she said, stricken. "Oh Andy." She went toward him, arms outstretched. They stood there holding each other. At some point, by mutual unspoken consent, they sank into the window seat and continued to sit, hugging each other like two children frightened of the dark.

"It's all right," he said at last, as though he were the one who needed to offer comfort. "It's the plague, all right, but it's not so terrible. I just don't seem to have any energy, that's the worst part. But I'm in no pain." He laughed. "I can get exhausted just getting downstairs from my bedroom. I should've known better than to think I could get to Harvard Square."

She couldn't believe the change. "It's only about ten months since I've seen you," she said incredulously.

"Yes. Things just galloped after I noticed the first lesion, which is not such a bad thing. For some people, it's long and slow, and I don't think I could bear that. I've been in discreet hiding for a couple of months."

She swallowed and looked out the window, blinking back tears. "How long . . . do you have?" she asked.

"Between three and six months, they think."

"God!" she said, shocked, her hands over her mouth.

He was so thin that the candlelight seemed to come right through his skin. His features, always fine and handsome, now had the eerie beauty of a changeling, of someone halfway between being and spirit.

"Marni," he said somberly, cupping her chin in his right hand and tilting her face toward the candelabra. For a weird second she was eighteen years old again, ten years ago, in the house in Jamaica Plain. Geraint had come for another look at her father's family icon, and had brought Anderson with him. Anderson Thorpe III. Even the name cast an aura. He was seventeen years older than she, and had traveled all over the world, and she and her father had both been spellbound. Anderson had taken her face in his hands and said: "You remind me of a painting in the Uffizi. A young Madonna by Fra Lippo Lippi." Marni had never heard of either the Uffizi, or of Fra Lippo Lippi, but she felt as though she were being touched by the hand of a god. She had wanted, suddenly and passionately, to enter that shining world of art and music and beauty where Anderson Thorpe lived. She had adored him.

Well, she still did, if it came to that.

"Marni," he said now, watching the candleshadow licking at her cheeks. "Do you have it too?"

"What?" she asked vaguely, surfacing from the glow of eighteen and innocence.

"Have you been tested?"

"What?" She frowned, trying to concentrate. "What are you talking about?"

He was searching her eyes. "Is that why you wanted to talk? Have you caught it from me?"

Her mouth fell open in astonishment. "Good God, Andy, how could—?"

"It's possible," he said. "There's such a lengthy incubation period, no one knows for sure how long it is. I've been terrified that you. . . . I'd never forgive myself if I'd made you. . . ."

"Andy!" She paced around the room, waving her arms, agitated. "Stop this nonsense this instant. As far as I know, I'm disgracefully healthy. But even if I weren't. . . . No one's responsible for a disease, for God's sake. A disease is a disease. It spreads, it strikes." She ran out of steam and sat down on the window seat again, facing him. "Andy," she said gently, "there are things you gave me that changed my life. I'll always be grateful. You taught me about art and music. You gave me, well, the realization that I could make choices. Make my own decision about what to be in life." She laughed a little incredulously. "If it hadn't been for you, I might have married some factory worker in Jamaica Plain, and still be living there, with six children and—"

"You might have been happier, Marni."

She looked at him sharply. "I'm happy, Andy. I like my life. And besides, you gave me the best thing of all, you gave me M—"

She stopped abruptly. Would it be a careless cruelty, a totally unnecessary shock, to tell him about Matthew now?

"What is it? Why did you want to see me?"

She bit her lip.

"I was sure you'd got wind of my condition," he said. "I was sure that was what it was about. I thought maybe Geraint had mentioned—"

"No," she said, a little startled. "I just saw him a couple of days ago, as a matter of fact, and he didn't give me the slightest—"

"Well, he wasn't supposed to, but I thought he might have accidentally. . . . The thing is, as you can imagine, I don't want Mother to know. It would break her heart, Marni, you know that." He stood and offered his arm, and led her to the dining table. "She's a formidable woman, but she's my mother. I don't want to hurt her." He rang for the housekeeper. "We'll have the soup now, Williams," he said.

Williams nodded. He came and went noiselessly on slippered feet.

Over an oyster bisque, Anderson said: "Geraint and I are leaving for Nice on the twenty-first of March. I'd like to die in the south of France." He grinned, almost boyishly. "Preferably sitting on a deck chair on those golden sands, watching the sun go down into the Mediterranean. Incurable romantic, that's my problem. Ever since I read *Death in Venice*, I think I've. . . . Anyway, it just seems to me the proper way to die."

"Andy," she said, choking on a mouthful of bisque. She dabbed at her eyes with the linen napkin. She was struck by the desolating fact that Eva lay drifting between life and death in Mass General, and now Andy. . . . "We may have the strangest ex-marriage on the books," she said, trying to joke, trying to match his determinedly flippant mood. "I've always thought of you as one of my best friends. You and Eva." Part of her mind was sifting other information. March twenty-first. And Geraint's surprise party was March twentieth. A farewell party. Was it generous or ghoulish of Geraint? With Geraint, one could never tell. "Funny, isn't it? I mean, it's not as though we see each other very often, but somehow I've. . . . You're so. . . . You're such a *good* person, Andy." She sniffled, and dabbed at her eyes with the napkin, and concentrated on several mouthfuls of bisque. "Sometimes I stand in my window and look down Mt. Vernon toward your place and. . . . Well, just knowing there's someone in the city who cares whether I'm. . . ." She gestured helplessly and gave up.

Anderson turned away and went to his CD player. He busied himself with putting a disk in position. "Mozart," he said, coming back to the table. "*The Magic Flute.* I play it all the time. These days I find Sarastro's hymn very comforting."

Williams came and took away the soup bowls, and brought the fish, a paupiette of sole.

"Andy," she said when he'd gone. "That man gives me the creeps."

"Bit moody, isn't he? I can never get two words out of him. It's just his way, I think. He's extremely conscientious. Geraint found him. It's not easy to get someone who'll, you know. . . . People are afraid."

"Geraint . . ." Marni began.

"I know you don't think much of him, Marni. But he's the most—"

"No, that's not—"

"—loyal friend I've got. Since we were ten years old. He was such a little ruffian." Andy smiled. "I was, you know, a mother's wimp when I arrived in school. Gerry defended me, he was always in fights. I've given him polish. And in return he's kept me safe. Always."

Marni concentrated on the sole and said nothing.

"You think I'm blind to his faults," Anderson said. "I'm not. I don't have any illusions about Gerry, he's what he is. He's promiscuous, or he used to be, I know that, but those affairs meant nothing to him. And the women. Well, we both do that for appearances. He doesn't get involved. He's always had his own kind of honor. The fact that he would never make a pass at you, for example."

Marni said carefully: "I've always known he was loyal to you, Andy."

"And he's been marvelous since I— I mean, it's only a matter of time till he gets it too, and yet there's never been a word of blame."

Marni stared at him, astonished. It would surely be the most supreme irony, or some joke of the gods, if Andy were to pass infection on to Geraint, and not the other way around. It seemed to her much more likely that Geraint was the carrier who had somehow escaped. . . . But what did she know? What did anyone know about this?

She said quietly, "I really don't see that blame has anything to do—"

"And it's due to him," Anderson said eagerly, "that it's been possible to keep this completely secret."

In the Back Bay? Marni wondered. "Andy, do you really think that's possible? Your mother must have some inkling. You can't keep something like this. . . ."

"Yes, you can," Anderson said. "You knew nothing, remember? I'll write to Mother from Nice. Something witty, so she'll have it to show. . . . With plans for the future, so it'll seem sudden, you see. I hope she'll never know the cause of my death."

What if she already knows? Marni wondered. What if she knows about Matthew? What bearing would one have on the other?

"I would have written to you too, Marni. Well, I still will. A farewell—the things it's easier to write than say." He raised his glass in a toast. "But I'm glad you know about all this now."

Me too, she thought. She found it difficult to speak.

"You know," he said, as though talk were flowing into him with the wine, "in the beginning, Mother adored you. She thought you were perfect. Oh, I know she didn't show it, that's not her way. But she did. She told me." Marni concentrated on the sole, which fell away from her fork in delicate flakes. "She thought it was the best thing I'd ever done, marrying you."

Marni reached for his hand and stroked it. "I thought so too, at the time, Andy. I've always loved you."

He turned away, and reached for the crystal decanter on the sideboard. He refilled their glasses. "If we'd managed to produce an heir," he sighed. "It would have been a good life, Marni. We could have kept up a good public front, lived our own lives in private."

But the cost of that, she remembered. The cost of acting a lie, of keeping up a good public front. She wondered how Anderson had possibly managed a lifetime of it.

"Do you ever fantasize," he asked—the tone was light, flippant—"about what a child of ours would have looked like? After all, we're both of us quite. . . . Our child would have looked like someone out of a Botticelli canvas." His laugh turned into something like a sob.

"And people think," he said, "that gays don't fantasize about having children. They think it's not an issue." He drank his wine rather quickly. Alarmingly so, Marni thought. "I'd give anything to have had a child," he said, a little thickly, the consonants beginning to slur. She stared at his pale, gaunt face. The eyes were cavernous, glittering, famished. He picked up a silver ladle from the table, an exquisite thing with a long handle of chased vines intertwined. He turned it over. "Coat of arms of the Bourbons," he said. "In the family since 1790. You think I don't want a child to give it to? I'd give anything. Anything."

"Andy," Marni said, feeling giddy.

"Yes?"

"There's something. . . ." She had to think. If she told him, his mother would have to know immediately. Then there was no way he would get out of the country without her seeing him. Would he want that? Also, if Marni told, there was the legal document that nestled, at this minute, in her coat pocket in the hallway. If she told, he still couldn't give the Bourbon silverware to his son. She'd already legally renounced all rights on Matthew's behalf. There was no way she'd change that. There was no way she would put up with Abigail insinuating that Marni had just wanted to get her hands on the family money; or have Abigail whisk Matthew out of his mother's custody and into some ritzy New England prep school.

Maybe it was better to say nothing. For just three more months, six at the most.

But what of the phone calls, the threats? What if Abigail already knew? What if Matthew was still in danger? Wouldn't it help to produce the legal document? Set Abigail's mind at rest? And wasn't there something immoral about not telling a dying man that he had a son?

Williams appeared suddenly, silently, and took the fish dishes away. Marni noted with a pang that Andy had hardly eaten a thing. The duck was served.

"You started to say something?" Anderson prompted.

Marni took a mouthful of wine and a deep breath. "Andy. . . ." Her throat was dry, her heart hammering. Then she said it in a rush: "You do have a son. He's five years old, and his name is Matthew."

Across the table and the candelabra they stared at each other. It was as though Circe had turned them both to stone. Ten seconds, twenty seconds. The words floated like alien objects in the sea of Anderson's mind, indecipherable, potent, shining. He was like a man afraid to come out of a trance.

She watched, holding her breath. He moved a hand jerkily, the way a patient does after a stroke, toward his wineglass. He drank another mouthful. His eyes never left her face.

She said softly: "He *is* beautiful, Andy. He looks like you in that portrait your mother has in the library. That one she had done when you first went away to school."

He was so still she was beginning to be frightened. Then he moved, lurched forward over the table, put his head in his hands. His body shook, but the sounds were muffled and low. She did not know whether to go to him or not. She was terrified Williams would come in.

"Andy?"

He didn't look up, but he held out a hand, and she went to him. He took her hand and kissed it. When he looked up, his face was wet but shining. The word *beatitude* fell into Marni's mind like a feather, twisting languidly.

"A son," he said. "A son." He kept shaking his head and gesturing with his hands as though searching for words to fit the discovery. "But where has he . . .? Why?"

"Andy, we couldn't have stayed married, it was impossible. You know it was. And I was afraid that if I—your mother. . . ."

"Yes," he said. "You're right about that. Where . . .? Can I see him?"

"Actually, he's in Mass General." There was a tremor in her voice. (Which circle was she in? Does this circle interlock with a dangerous one?) "He'll be all right, but he's been in an accident. I don't think it's a good idea. . . ."

"No," he said wistfully. "I don't go out much. I try not to be seen."

"But I could bring him here for a visit as soon as. . . . "

"Yes." He brightened. "Do you have a picture?"

"Of course." She took them from her wallet and showed him.

He went over to the window seat and looked at them one by one. He seemed suddenly full of energy. He walked up and down the room, stopped to look at the photographs again, resumed his pacing. He sat down, facing her, his eyes bright.

"This changes things, Marni. Listen to me. I've already drawn up a will that leaves you a generous sum. But the bulk of my estate I was leaving to—"

"Andy, before you go any further," she interrupted. "Listen to me. This is not something open to negotiation. Wait here. I've got something to show you. I'll just be a second." Her movement toward the hallway where her coat hung was quiet and sudden, which explained why Williams had no warning. When Marni opened the dining-room door, there was a resistance, a sense of collision, the thunderous clatter of falling tray and plates.

"Jesus bloody Christ!" Williams shouted, in involuntary shock. "Watch your step, you stupid idiot!"

Marni froze, terrified: the muted British accent, the faintly burred lisp on the *s* sounds. She flattened herself against the wall, paralyzed, as Williams got to his feet. He was waiting there, she thought. Behind the door. Listening.

"What is it? What is it?" Andy was saying, startled, coming toward them.

(Was it genuine, Andy's surprise? Marni felt the dizziness, the terror, of someone who knows that nothing can be counted on. Absolutely nothing. Black is white, clear is muddy, safe is dangerous.)

She fled down the hallway and grabbed her coat and boots. There was no time to put them on. Clutching them as best she could, she rushed down the stairs to the street.

12: Jake's Sunday

Sunday was Jake's turn for the kids. Judy dropped them at the curb outside his apartment building in Charlestown, and he watched through the window as his sons were swallowed up by the front porch. Kathy was getting instructions from her mother, hopping from one foot to the other on the snowy sidewalk while her mother talked to her through the car window. That would be Jake Junior pressing and pressing on the buzzer.

He went downstairs to let them in.

Brian affected heavy obligation and boredom, and did not respond to his father's hug.

"Mommy wants to see you," Kathy said.

"Go on up," he told the kids, and braced himself for Judy, who was watching from the car. He slipped on the steps, which no one ever shoveled. Forget seeing a landlord in Charlestown. The path to the gate was a series of ridged wavelets, snow packed down by footprints, frozen into size tens, size fourteens, a moon walk. Crater Way. He slipped again on the sidewalk.

"I don't want them tired out," Judy said. "Kathy's been to the doctor for a sore throat this week."

"You didn't mention it Thursday." He couldn't believe that was less than three days ago, Sister Agatha, the drawings, the bungled moment with Brian. It all seemed faint and distant, all that mayhem in between, and the night in the apartment on Mt. Vernon Street. . . . His mind slid away, not wanting to submit his frail pleasures to Judy's accusing eyes. He'd forgotten, he'd actually forgotten about Brian. There was the problem, he thought guiltily. He agreed with Judy's verdict: *We just don't exist for you half the time.* He wondered if he'd been defective right from the beginning. And was he raising (or failing to raise) a son just like himself?

"I want them home in bed early," Judy said. "I'll be back at five on the dot."

"Sure." He rested his arms on her window ledge and bent toward her. "Things okay with you?"

"What would you care?" she said, slipping the clutch.

He took the kids out to the Burlington Mall, where Jake Junior rode Puff the Magic Dragon fifteen times. In the toy store they lingered for an hour, trying everything, playing the wish game. Thank God for Sunday opening. They stopped to watch a man who was a whiz with a stick of charcoal. He drew pictures of people for five dollars.

"You could do that, Brian," Jake said. "You're better than he is." There. He'd said it. "Much better," he emphasized. "I think you're terrific."

Brian flashed him a quick startled look, and was unable to repress a smile, though he clearly tried to.

Can we, Dad? Can we? Kathy and Jake Junior asked. Have our picture drawn?

Jake paid for two drawings. Kathy's really looked like her. Jake Junior's did not, and he burst into tears.

"It's not me," he sobbed. "I don't like that man."

The artist, nettled, said: "Divorce makes for disturbed kids, doesn't it?"

Disturbed kids. The word set up odd vibrations. Jake gritted his teeth. "What makes you think I'm divorced?"

The charcoal artist raised his eyebrows in a manner that implied: Isn't it obvious?

Jake Junior tore his drawing in half. "I hate you," he told the charcoal man.

"I'm sorry," Jake apologized to the artist. "Here, can I buy a stick of charcoal and a sheet of art paper from you?"

"Sure," the artist said with considerable hostility. "Keep the little brat amused, right?"

While Jake Junior was being consoled with a Dairy Queen, Jake got Brian to draw his little brother.

"Wow," Kathy said. "That's good."

"It's me," Jake Junior said. "Gimme, gimme, it's me."

Brian didn't want to give up his drawing. "I'll look after it," he said.

Jake Junior sniffled, woebegone.

"You're such a cry baby," Kathy chided.

Jake Junior punched her.

"Kathy's eyes look puffy," was all Judy said later. "I just hope her fever's not up tonight."

"Brian's done an excellent drawing of little Jake." He was conciliatory, pleading a bit. "I've told him we think he has enormous talent."

"Good for you," Judy snapped. "I wonder why Jake Junior's always so cranky when he's spent the day with you."

"Will you come in for a cup of tea?"

"No," she said, revving the engine.

He got back inside his apartment and took a beer out of the fridge and sat in front of the television set with his feet up. *Disturbed kids.* He didn't turn the set on. Disturbed. Something disturbed him. He wanted to think, though the memory of Marni Verstak's perfume kept interfering.

At six o'clock he called her, but got no answer. At the hospital, probably. Or wasn't she going to visit her ex? He picked up the phone book and looked up her ex's name. Unlisted, naturally. God. He was acting like a high-school kid.

Disturbed kids. . . .

A word kept bothering him. *Disturbed.*

Mr. Lisp on the call they'd both listened to: *You're not disturbed, are you?*

Something about that, but he couldn't quite put his finger on what. It was like trying to remember a dream that's just slithered off the sheets and gone under the edge of the mattress. The word was settling somewhere deep in his mind, sinking down, a stone through a pond. It was giving off powerful vibes. When it found its level, he'd be able to translate. He'd have the dream by the tail.

For now what came back were their heads (his and hers) side by side, the receiver between them. The British voice with the lisp. Jake was concentrating, memorizing, listening for every nuance and clue. But he was also conscious that the knuckles of his hand, the one holding the receiver, were touching her cheek. He was conscious of her perfume, her hair, a desire to stroke it. The look in her eyes, partly fear. And partly relief.

I *did* get those phone calls.

And then he had it. Dr. Ainsley Wilson. "Ainsley thinks I might have imagined the phone calls. Ainsley says it's not uncommon, that kind of thing, in anxiety disorders." And in a wry, half embarrassed, half self-mocking tone: "You know, for disturbed people like me."

And the nighttime caller: *You're not disturbed, are you?*

It might mean nothing. His gut told him it meant a lot.

The phone rang. "Yes?" he said, leaping on it.

"Got something on your man." It was Big Turk's voice.

"Which one?"

"Your Mr. Lisp," Big Turk said.

"Yes?"

"Kinky. Special sexual services for the very rich, AC/DC, preferably SM, privacy of your own home. That kind of thing. Also a bagman. Discreet deliveries of hash and coke to exclusive addresses, C.O.D. But I don't see any tie to your rainbow car."

"Got names of his clients?"

"I'm working on that. I'll get a list."

"Thanks. Another thing. Can you get me any info on a Dr. Ainsley Wilson, psychotherapist, office in Copley Square? Anything on her at all."

"I'll get back to you tomorrow."

Special sexual services for the very rich. Discreet deliveries to exclusive addresses. Jake hunkered down inside the details and thought.

When he next noticed the time it was late, eleven o'clock, and Marni would probably be back from dinner with her ex. He'd check just to see she was okay. There was no answer. Stupidly, he let the phone ring and ring, at least twenty times, before he gave up.

Much of the night, Jake paced his apartment, mentally replaying Mr. Lisp's call. *I hope I'm not frightening you. You're not disturbed, are you?*

He was still burrowing down inside the details.

He fell asleep on his sofa. In his dream, Marni was sitting on a bench in a garden, beside a tree. There was a snake, a little garden snake, in the grass near her feet. He hit it with a stick and killed it. A second later, to his chagrin, he saw it still crawling toward her. It was twice as big. He whacked it again. It slithered on, getting fatter and longer with every undulation across the grass. With his nightstick, he beat it to a pulp. He picked it up on the point of his stick and tossed it over his shoulder.

"It's all right now," he said.

He turned around and was eye to eye with the snake. It was big as a python, coiled around the tree trunk, its long neck swaying toward him, its forked tongue flicking in and out.

"I hope I'm not frightening you," it said. "You're not disturbed, are you?"

13: Marni's Sunday Night

Stumbling along the poorly shoveled sidewalk toward Massachusetts Avenue, Marni watched for a taxi. Beacon Street was clogged with parked cars and it seemed to her that a mugger lurked behind every one. She darted through a space beside a fire hydrant and ran down the middle of the street. If anything was going to happen, she wanted to be out in the open. Ahead, there was plenty of traffic on Mass Ave., but no pedestrians, and not a single taxi to be seen. Sunday, bloody Sunday, in the prim Back Bay.

She was freezing, her teeth chattering, her shoes packed with spiky, semi-frozen snow, but a wave of primitive fear kept her from stopping to pull on her coat or change into her boots. Patches of black ice on the road lay in wait like traps. She slithered and slipped and lurched. Once she fell and jarred her wrist badly as she thrust out her hand to break her fall.

The liquor store on the corner, closed, beckoned as a port in the storm. She stumbled gratefully into the alcove of its doorway, out of the wind, but outlined by a protective glare of ghostly neon. Coat, boots, warmth, it was a survival drumbeat in her mind. She found one sleeve and then—

Panic. Harm was everywhere, Williams had her, it was hopeless. . . . She bit on the woolen sleeve to keep from screaming. (*Stop it, stop it, you're out of control, you're freaking out!*)

"Shitshitshit," a voice mumbled thickly. "Watch where yer fucking stepping, bitch."

There was a man huddled in the doorway. He stank of cheap whiskey. She saw, from the neon haze and the intermittent passing

133

headlights, that he was in no condition to molest her. He was rocking himself back and forth, muttering, staring at the cement floor between his feet, while she put on her coat, stuffed her shoes into its pockets, pulled on her boots. Her heart was still thudding, her eyes scanning the street for a taxi.

Why is it that the times when your safety, maybe your life, depend on quick decisions—why is that the very time when an unnatural calm, a state of shock, descends? Part of her mind, a sleepwalker part, in slow motion, considered this philosophical problem, turned it over and over like a curious object, to get the light.

Another part kept watch like an animal at bay. Yellow cab! She saw it and dashed out between traffic, arm high, waving frantically. But the cab already had a passenger and did not pause. This was like being trapped in a nightmare. She kept half running along Mass Ave. at the edge of the curb, at the rim of her nightmare, stumbling more or less backwards so she could face the oncoming traffic, watching for cabs. She collided with someone and gave a small stifled scream.

"Any spare change?" The man wore only a thin denim jacket, jeans, and sneakers. He held his folded arms across his chest, and shivered while he watched her. "Fifty cents? C'd do with a cup of coffee."

"Um," she said, afraid to stop. And then from the corner of her eye, she saw another cab and rushed out and hailed it.

It slowed. It stopped. *Oh thank God, thank God.*

"Fuck *you*," the man on the sidewalk said as she got in. But he said it listlessly, without energy or anger, the way he might have said: It's still night, it's still cold, it's still snowing.

She bit her lip and wound down the window to hand out fifty cents, fumbling for her purse. *Her purse!* She'd left it at Andy's.

"Haven't got all night," the taxi driver said, moving sharply forward. "Where to?"

She felt frantically in her coat pocket. Thank God her keys were there. She'd have to go inside for money to pay for the taxi.

"Do you know where you're going or not, ma'am?" the taxi driver asked sarcastically.

Marni gave her address. She looked out the back window. The man on the sidewalk simply stood there and hugged himself and shivered.

In the doorway behind him, another man huddled. And in the next doorway too. And the next. And the next.

In the back of the taxi, Marni also hugged herself and shivered. The world is horrible, she thought. Horrible. A very unsafe place. She couldn't sort out any of what had happened. All her senses, her bodily and visceral responses, were on red alert. But her thoughts were on hold, the machine that made thinking possible was on the blink. Get home, get inside, get safe, her survival instincts said. Where's home, where's safe? came an answering drumbeat. She felt as though she were one with the drifters on the street: nowhere to go, no one to trust.

But of course that was ridiculous. Pull yourself together, a reflex ordered. Her taxi was climbing the steep slope of Mt. Vernon Street, the most proper street in Boston, surely one of the safest. The gas lamps lit up gracious Federal doorways and bays, Greek Revival arcades, leaded fanlights. Across from Louisburg Square, the taxi stopped.

"Look," she said, "I'm terribly sorry, but I've lost my handbag. I'll have to ask you to wait here for a minute while I run upstairs and get money to pay you."

The taxi driver swore under his breath.

She had to clamber over a snowbank to get to her door. There were two locks, requiring both keys, on the outer door; then the small mailbox lobby, then another door, requiring another key, into the main lobby. Triply protected, she thought, fumbling with keys turned suddenly perverse. Triply sealed off from help, triply tricked, triple dipple, deep shit, triply tipply. She felt mildly hysterical and began giggling, then crying (one or the other) as she jiggled a key that could care less.

Please, she said to it. Please.

It turned. The door opened. The main lobby was its usual musty-smelling, deserted self.

She took the elevator, which was old and ponderous and slow. It must have been in the running for the oldest elevator in the country, she thought. It could take a maximum load of four persons. It stopped opposite her door on the fourth floor. Another two locks, two keys.

As she turned the second key, she heard her phone ringing.

She ignored it, grabbed a fistful of quarters from the laundry-money jar in the kitchen cupboard, locked the apartment door again, took the elevator back down. "I'm awfully sorry," she said, as she poured a small avalanche of coins into the driver's hand. She had to bite on her lip to keep the panic at bay as he gunned the engine and drove off.

The locks were just as resistant as last time, the elevator just as slow, the phone still ringing—or ringing again—as she unlocked her own door.

Her heart leaped so wildly, she thought her chest muscles might go into cramp. She got through her door, slammed it shut, turned the dead bolts, hands shaking. She leaned against the door and watched the phone. *Breathe deeply, slowly, count to ten.* The phone's tantrum went on and on.

(*Answer*, Jake pleaded silently, at the other end.)

Don't panic, Marni told herself. *Think.*

As though she were approaching a live hand grenade with its pin pulled, she tiptoed across the room, reached for the wall jack, and pulled it out.

Merciful silence.

Her whole body was shaking. She did not dare take her eyes off the blind beyond which the fire escape lay. Somebody, please, she whispered, not even aware that she was crying soundlessly. She switched on every light in the apartment and sat watching the window for the rest of the night. Her mind was numb. She explained the rules to herself: if I don't let the window and the fire escape out of my sight, not even to blink, I'll be safe.

If only she knew how to reach Jake Murphy in the middle of the night. Suppose she called the emergency number at the police department? But what would she say? I've found the person who's been making threatening phone calls about my son. But her son was safely in a hospital bed, and an undercover cop was keeping watch at the ward.

So what would she say?

I'm in a mindless state of abject panic. I'm afraid of shadows. Could you send Jake Murphy around to hold me?

If she called Ainsley, she'd get the answering service. Would Dr. Ainsley Wilson be any help? *The ego boundaries of disturbed people ... disturbed people think everything is happening to them personally.*

I'm crazy, Marni thought. I'm a basket case.

She felt less and less certain that Williams's voice was the voice of the telephone caller. She felt less and less certain that he'd spoken at all.

She thought of nothing, there were blanks where thoughts might have been, though images, like frames from a silent movie, kept flickering across the surface of her mind: Matthew in his hospital bed, Eva hooked up to her tubes, Anderson looking at the photographs of his son. She thought dully: *I left them there. When I ran out to the hallway, I left the photographs in the dining room with Andy.*

And the legal document?

She had forgotten all about it. Not letting the window out of her sight, she felt in her coat pocket. It was still there. Tomorrow, she would try to think what to do with it. Tomorrow, she would try to figure out what everything meant. For now, the power of thinking was beyond her. Only the images kept flickering by, a never-ending show: Matthew, Eva, Andy, Williams the silent butler. She kept seeing the sullen face of Williams, seeing him on the floor in the hallway; she kept trying to replay his voice. Had she imagined it? Was she paranoid? She saw the homeless men huddled in doorways along Mass Ave. Joseph Lucyk leaned out of every alcove, handing her his sad bit of doggerel verse. Joseph Lucyk lay bloodied in the snow.

When dawn trickled through the window blinds at last, she set her alarm and slept raggedly for an hour. In her dream, endless lines of homeless men filed by. Can you spare a house, ma'am? they asked. Can you spare a bit of warmth, a bit of safety? They all had the face of Joseph Lucyk. Well, fuck you, they all said. Give up on the house, let it go. What do you care? You're warm.

But not safe, she cried. Not safe, not safe. Don't you understand, Joseph? I tried, but what more can I possibly do?

Joseph Lucyk said nothing, he just went on bleeding, there were bubbles of blood at his throat.

14: Monday Morning

On Monday morning, Marni woke exhausted.

At nine o'clock, she called the Boston City Police Department and asked for the Special Drug Task Force. Then for Sergeant Murphy. He wasn't there, and she had to leave a message.

She took a cab to the hospital. Matthew was awake, and she sat and held his hand and listened to his sweet, meandering prattle. He spoke of the tree house that he and Deszo were building. Mercifully, he seemed to have no recollection of the crash. A nurse came and said Marni had to go.

In the hallway, she tried to ascertain which of the people was the security guard promised by Jake Murphy. No one seemed a likely candidate. But then, an undercover cop is not supposed to look like one. She watched the nurses and orderlies who came and went from Eva's room, from the children's room. Any one of them could have been working for Williams, how would she know? How would Jake's security guard know?

She forced herself to stop thinking about this, and took a cab to her office.

"Hey!" Roger looked at her strangely when she went by him. I must be quite a sight, she thought. "Here a minute," he called. "Have to talk to you." She was still operating on automatic pilot and a residue of adrenaline.

Roger said: "Where the hell have you been?"

Her eyes widened. She was too taken aback to speak.

"Been trying to get hold of you for two days," he said. "Where've you been, for Chrissake?"

138

"The hospital mostly." Why was he asking? They never had to account for their comings and goings, unless they missed a strategy meeting. They were free agents, and only the bottom line counted. "My, uh . . . a friend of mine's in critical. I left a message Friday, didn't you get it?"

"Just the same," he said irritably. "Next time you get an employee stabbed and get our company into the papers—"

"What?"

"—appreciate it if you'd stick around to answer questions. Goddam reporters, nothing better to do, don't sic 'em onto me next time." He thrust the city's tabloid in front of her. "Pack of wolves."

The page-two headline read: DRUGS, DEATHS, KICKBACKS IN CITY'S REAL ESTATE WARS. There was a picture of Marni in front of the Jamaica Plain house. She was flanked by Alonso and Jacobson. The caption read: "Wheeler-dealer and would-be developer Verstak (center) first declines comment, disappears." Marni stared at the picture, one of the final acts of Joseph Lucyk's life. How had the newspaper got hold of it? There was a smaller, separate picture of Michael (Irregularities, leaks, lawyer claims) and one of Roger (Shocked, broker says.)

"Says somewhere in there," Roger growled, "that you fled the state to escape prosecution."

"What?"

"This reporter tracks you down to a Hertz office in Harvard Square. He calls me. Wants to know if we're bag running for some syndicate. Jesus!" Marni's head spun, the room swayed queasily, she had to hang onto the arm of the chair. "I said we did that all the time, made trips out of state for clients, check out country houses, that kinda thing."

"Rog, this whole thing is—"

"Hard to explain the goddamn rental car, though." He swept his arm across his desk, knocking a spike file onto the floor. "I mean, when you have a car of your own sitting in the Exeter Street garage." He got up, plunked the spike file back on his desk in a way that suggested it was her fault it had fallen off. "Specially," he said heavily, closing his office door behind her, "when you don't answer the phone, return my calls. What'sa matter, you never listen to your answering machine, or what?"

Marni slumped in a chair across from him. Even words seemed to her dangerous now, unreliable. Where would she begin?

"Look, Marni," Roger said, clearing his throat. He rearranged pens and paper on the desk in front of him. "Look, those jackals in the press. . . . I know damn well half of this is a crock of shit, but the thing is. . . ."

She could feel herself going numb, being very, very calm. The thing was: she had caught some kind of unreal but deadly disease. The worst you could imagine (no, worse than that; stuff it would never have occurred to you to imagine) was going to go on happening to her, like a degenerative disease.

"Of course I'm sympathetic, on the personal level," Roger was saying. "Whatever it is you've got mixed up in. But there's a limit, you know. I can't let the company go down the tubes, I draw the line there, understand?"

Marni was watching his hands, the way they fidgeted with pens and paper clips.

"When Mike told me who was behind the offer to purchase on your pet project, well, you could've knocked me over with a feather, Marni."

She leaned forward slightly. She wanted to ask, with a sleepwalker's calm curiosity: "What are you talking about?" But something had happened to the connections between her brain and the rest of her bodily functions. Her mouth moved like a fish's mouth, comic, silent.

"I'm not saying it's treason, mind you. Don't agree with Michael there, though I gotta admit, evidence is pretty damning. But we go back a coupla years, huh? Good years, you've brought in business, gotta hand it to you."

A paper clip suddenly popped out of his fingers like a missile and zinged past Marni's arm. "Just as tough for me," he was saying. "Jesus, never thought I'd have to. . . . Effective immediately, best all round, I think, don't you?"

"Roger," she said very quietly, "are you asking for my resignation?"

"You're not listening, Marni. Think of it as a month's leave. Not saying it can't be opened up again in the future," he blustered, looking away. "When the dust settles. All depends."

"I would like to know," she said, "what Michael said about the offer to purchase. Because the only one I know about was from a black deli owner. And that was verbal. He couldn't even submit a formal offer unless we could get some form of financial support. He doesn't meet conventional mortgage requirements, the banks wouldn't touch him."

"Yeah," Roger said sarcastically. "I been reading about it." He tapped the tabloid. "Drug cartel, pressure on city council, kickbacks. Deli owner, huh? That's what he told you?" He threw up his hands in a gesture that meant: how naive, how stupid can you get? "Through the crack in his shop window, about as close as he'd get to the deli business." He laughed shortly at his own pun. "Sour *crack*, not sauerkraut, Marni. And the deli owner's wife just happens to be a secretary for Olde Pilgrim."

A silly jingle kept going through Marni's mind like a cracked record: *Round and round the mulberry bush, the monkey chased the weasel.* Roger, she wanted to ask, are we both in someone else's nightmare? Her mind was reaching through cotton wool for logic.

"Roger," she said earnestly. "If my buyer was in drugs, he'd be loaded with cash. Why would he need the banks or the city for mortgage money? And another thing, I don't understand how Michael—"

"Look, Marni, like I said. Pack of wolves, those jerks." He tapped the tabloid again. "Three quarters of it bullshit, I'm in your corner, kid. But until things get sorted out. . . . We'll talk when the storm blows over, okay? But I can't just let the company, hell, you wouldn't want me to, right? We've both worked too hard. So here's your statement for the press. Sign and no hard feelings, huh?"

Marni looked him in the eyes and he looked away. "I'll start packing things up in my office," she said.

"Shit, Marni, don't make things— For Chrissake, there's no need to get on your high horse. Just leave stuff be, just stay away from the office for a month or so, then if everything's blown over. . . . Well, that's all I'm—"

"Sure, Roger," she said quietly, leaving.

But once she got to her own office, it was all she could do not to put her head on the desk and sob. Instead she dialed the Drug Task Force again. Could she speak to Sergeant Murphy?

Sergeant Murphy was not in the office at present. Would she leave a message? She did so for the second time. She wanted to add: tell him it's urgent. She thought of the number of bodies he must see each week, against which she could offer: a newspaper is slinging mud at me, a man I once made love to has told my boss I'm guilty of treason, I got more or less fired, I think I found the man who made the nasty telephone calls, I want a shoulder to cry on, I want to be held. No, she could not, in good conscience, claim that her need for him was urgent.

Mechanically, she began taking books down from her shelves, stacking them. Once she looked up to find Michael watching her through the doorway. She thought of asking *Why?* but it seemed irrelevant. He was a total stranger. It was difficult to remember why she had ever felt anything for him. Michael's look seemed to mean something, but she could not read it.

At nine on Monday morning, Jake was in Ainsley Wilson's suite, talking to her receptionist. He did not check with his office first, he did not pass go, he did not collect his messages.

He was riding the crest of an obsession.

"Special Branch," he said, showing his badge. "Drug Task Force. I'd like to have a few words with Dr. Wilson."

The receptionist was startled. On the intercom, her voice shook a little.

"She'll see you now," the receptionist said.

Thus it was that Jake did not see the morning's tabloids with their pictures of Marni and their rumors of scandal, he did not get his phone messages from Marni, and he was not in his office when news came in on a homicide in a Beacon Street mansion.

15: A Very Proper Death

Marni went on methodically emptying her desk drawers, packing the contents into liquor-store cartons. She said to herself: Now I'll be able to sit beside Matthew's bed all the time until he's released. In her dazed and disconnected state, this seemed like a stroke of good fortune. She wouldn't let him out of her sight. She'd keep him safe. Then she'd be able to stay home with him. For a few weeks, she decided, I won't even approach another company, I'll just stay home. We'll spend all our time together, I'll read him stories, take him to see the frozen pond in the Public Garden. Mentally, she began converting her study on Mt. Vernon Street into a room for Matthew. I'll have to get a larger condo, she thought.

When she looked up and saw the two police officers with Roger in her doorway, she felt a dizzy, cavernous space opening up inside her. She put out a hand and clutched at her desk to keep from falling. She waited for bad news about her son.

It had nothing to do with Matthew.

Once that was established, Marni felt a sort of supernatural calm. She thought to herself, very logically, very precisely, that she should have been working more quickly. If she'd been more efficient with her packing, she would have been home, or back at the hospital by now.

She would have preferred not to have been arrested at the office.

She intimated this to the officers. "I should have worked faster," she said.

They were quite courteous, the officers, and she went with them as though she were a princess on an escorted tour. There were no

143

handcuffs, nothing like that. With an officer on each side of her, she walked past the secretaries, head held high.

When the very worst happens, she thought, it's almost easy. All that's left, all that's *possible*, is going down with style. Be polite. Look serene when your head is on the block. As one of Henry the Eighth's wives said to the axman: Could you please pin my hair up out of the ·vay?

She walked past Michael's office and their eyes met. She thought she saw fear, a begging look. Then she thought it was something else, something nastier: *You had it coming.* Or perhaps: *If you'd played by my terms, none of this would have happened.* Then again, it might have been horror in his eyes. Or maybe all of those things at one and the same time. She couldn't read anything anymore.

Roger said something, but the sound never got to her. Or came jumbled, like airport announcements. Whatever. She couldn't decode what he said.

She got into the car, between the two officers. There were people with cameras on the sidewalk, shutters clicking like crazy. She nodded politely toward them, like a queen, very gracious.

One of the reporters wedged his foot in the car door and leaned right into the car. "Did you poison your ex-husband at dinner?" he asked. "Or after?"

And other voices shouted: "The real estate scandal. . . ."

"Blackmail? Hush money from the family? Did your ex refuse . . .?"

"Was he planning to remarry? Cut you out of the will?"

"No comment at this time," one of the officers said, pulling the car door shut.

"Do you know Jake?" she asked him.

She couldn't remember if he answered or not. In the precinct office, while they pressed her fingers on the ink pad, she asked him again. And then again, when he held out her handbag.

"You have the right to remain silent," he said. "Do you recognize this?"

"It's my purse," she said. "I left it at Andy's last night." The officer let her look through it. Everything was there but the photographs of Matthew. She thought it better not to mention them.

"Do you know Jake?" she asked the officer again when she was charged with the murder of Anderson Thorpe. "Could you give him a message?"

"Sure," the officer said. But the way he said it, she was not confident that he really did know Jake.

A VERY PROPER DEATH was how the tabloid reporter headed his copy. You never knew, of course, if the editor would keep your title. Nine times out of ten, he didn't. Nine times out of ten, a headline rose into the editor's mind like froth, like champagne on the spill. It might or might not have anything to do with your copy. You weren't supposed to care. Sleaze sold, sex sold, violence sold, and murder most certainly sold. A very classy murder at a very classy address was a godsend. Your editor could say: that was the headline that grabbed the attention that sold the paper that brought in the buck that paid for your story that wowed your editor that thought up the headline that grabbed the attention, et cetera.

The reporter had a hunch that this time his title might stick, but just to be sure he added a subhead: Boston Brahmin poisoned; beautiful ex-wife in custody. (You had to be careful how you put the murder and the suspect together. You weren't allowed to say she did it. The newspaper's lawyers were vultures for that kind of thing.)

He was rushing to make the evening edition. The copy read:

Early this morning, police were called to a mansion on Beacon Street in the Back Bay. The call was made by a hysterical cleaning lady who had found the body of her employer, wealthy socialite and playboy Anderson Thorpe III, dead in his bed. The room was undisturbed. There were no signs of struggle or theft. The deceased was sitting up in bed propped on damask pillows, wearing wine-colored silk pyjamas, a glass of half drunk sherry on his night table. The reading lamp was still on, and *Life Studies*, a book of poetry by Robert Lowell, was still in his hands.

In the dining room, there was evidence of a gourmet dinner for two. The table was set with fine china, silverware, crystal, and candelabra. The dessert, a lime sherbet, was still melting in Waterford bowls.

A handbag containing the usual pieces of personal identification was left on a chair in the dining room. Police identified the owner of the purse as businesswoman and real-estate wheeler-dealer Marni Verstak, former wife of Thorpe. The Thorpe marriage was annulled six years ago, after four years of what, on the surface of things, was believed to be connubial bliss. Reason for the annulment was widely believed to be Verstak's inability to produce an heir. Earlier this week, Verstak's name was mentioned in connection with City Council kickbacks in a real-estate scandal. Arrested at her office and taken into custody this morning, Verstak nodded almost light-heartedly to reporters but refused to answer questions.

A forensic expert who asked not to be identified said he expected that traces of strong sedative would be found in Thorpe's coffee cup on the dinner table, and that he expected poison to have been administered via the glass of sherry. Verstak's fingerprints were on the glass, the spokesman said.

Verstak claims to have taken fright because of a servant or valet, and to have fled from the house before dinner was over. She claims to have taken a taxi home. There is no corroborating evidence for this, police said. There are no fingerprints on the dinnerware other than those of Thorpe and Verstak.

Asked for her reaction to finding the body of her employer, cleaning lady Adela Gerassi crossed herself and said a prayer in Italian.

The deceased's mother, prominent Boston Brahmin hostess and patron of the arts Abigail Thorpe, could not be reached for comment on the untimely death of her son.

Social acquaintances said the estranged couple were on cordial terms, and that it was widely believed that Mr. Thorpe had named Verstak generously in his will. However, one acquaintance suggested, this might have been subject to recent change. Mr. Thorpe, a dealer in silverware and antiques as well as one of the city's most eligible bachelors, has not been seen around town since he returned from Italy before Christmas. There were rumors of a

love interest in Venice. It is thought that he was planning to
remarry.

A police spokesman who asked not to be identified said possible
motives for the murder were jealousy or matters related to the
substantial Thorpe inheritance.

(A day later, when the tabloid article appeared, Marni's
first thought was: Thank God, for dear Andy's sake, they didn't
mention AIDS.

Her second thought was: But the lesions? AIDS was surely obvious to
the police.

Had the details been suppressed by Abigail, who would certainly
have that sort of power? Or before they reached her, by someone else?
For Andy's sake, Marni hoped it was the latter.)

"Would you like to call your lawyer now?" the officer asked.

Marni thought about the word. *Lawyer.* Images came to mind:
Michael Lavan in her blue floral sheets when she brought in his
morning coffee; Michael Lavan's wife sobbing and accusing on the
phone; Michael saying: "My wife's thrown a tantrum, we'll have to be
more careful"; Michael telling Roger that Marni leaked information to
the enemy; Michael watching as the police led her past his office.

"No," she said, almost drowsily. "I don't think so."

"But you—you're supposed to call the lawyer of your choice."

She had another lawyer, didn't she? Yes. The one who drew up the
legal renunciation of inheritance. (Where *was* that? Coat pocket? No.
She'd taken it out, left it in her apartment.) What was that lawyer's
name? She couldn't think of it. "I think I'd rather have Jake," she said.
"Is this where Jake works?"

"Jake? He's your lawyer of choice? You got the last name and
number?"

"I thought he worked here," she said vaguely.

The two officers looked at each other. One of them scratched
his head.

"Um," he said, awkward, chivalrous. "Can I get you coffee or something?"

She smiled at him. "That would be very nice."

Down the hallway, he said to his colleague: "In shock, I think."

His colleague said: "Or crackers. Not guilty by reason of, et cetera."

The first one said: "Lay you ten to one she's not guilty, period."

"Just a sucker for a pretty face," his companion laughed.

She'd never seen the inside of a cell before. It was small and certainly not attractive.

"Don't you have somewhere else?" she asked the warden, a woman with ample hips and short spiky hair.

"Jesus," the warden said.

Marni sat on the bed, huddled up against the wall. The mattress was thin and hard, worse than a motel mattress. There was no bedspread, just a horrid green blanket with a rough ropy surface. She hugged herself and stared into the cement corridor.

There were black lines, like pickets, running from ceiling to floor.

She thought of picket fences. When she was a little girl, there was a picket fence in front of the house in Jamaica Plain. Roses and peonies in the front and a vegetable patch in the back. There was also an elm with a tire swing hanging from its lowest branch.

She supposed there wasn't a single elm left in the whole of Jamaica Plain now. And maybe not a single picket fence either. That was the worst thing about the present. It was horrible. It was very dangerous. She much preferred the past.

She is seven years old, sitting inside the old tire, swooping back and forth under the elm tree. Her father is pushing the swing.

"Close your eyes and make a wish," he says.

She closes her eyes.

When she opened them, there was the warden again, wanting to take her somewhere. Things happened, people came and went, there was an arraignment, formal charges were read. No—Marni shook her head—she had nothing to say. Then she was back in her cell, eyes closed, wishing. This time it worked. When she opened her eyes, the warden was there with a visitor.

"Marni," he said. "How absolutely unconscionable of these clowns. I've paid your bail. Now we'll have to get this muddle sorted out."

"Geraint." She was glad to see him, an old friend, the past coming back. Once he'd come to the house in Jamaica Plain, when the picket fence was still standing, and brought Anderson with him. And her father had beamed, and had shown them the treasured icon. When the warden unlocked the door and Geraint put his arms around her, she rested her head gratefully on his shoulder. "Someone killed Andy," she whispered.

"Yes, it's awful. Awful," Geraint said.

"I didn't do it," she said.

"Of course you didn't." The very slight wandering of Geraint's right eye touched her. It was such a slight thing, an almost cast, but it seemed to register his distress about Andy.

She frowned a little, puzzled, trying to remember something. "There was a horrible man, the housekeeper—"

"Don't try to talk now," he said. "You're in shock. I'll take you home."

16: Analyzing the Analyst

"You must understand, Sergeant Murphy," Dr. Ainsley Wilson said, "that this interruption of clinical time is a very serious matter." Her elbows were on the desk, and she was adjusting the ring on her right hand with the fingers of her left. The stone in the ring was a large diamond, clear and icy. He did not think the hand movement was an unconscious gesture, although it was meant to look like one. She was gracious and polite. The adjustment of the ring was meticulous, reminding him of the way expert safecrackers worked on difficult combination locks. "My receptionist will have to shuffle the day's appointments, and the possible repercussions for patients. . . ." Her sigh and the mournful shake of her head invited him to envisage breakdowns, suicides, mayhem. She now touched fingertips to fingertips, tenting her hands, so that the spire was just below her chin. Her hands were immaculately manicured. She was not a woman, he thought, inclined to let any splinter of detail slip out of her control. Her eyes looked directly into his as she let the full weight of his moral culpability sink in. Then she brushed her dark hair back from one shoulder and lifted a conveniently straying curl from her forehead. It was the kind of orchestrated performance (rehearsed, perhaps, before private mirrors?) that he had seen over and over again in courtrooms, and she did it well. "So you can appreciate, perhaps," she said, "my astonishment at this unorthodox intrusion. And my hope that you do have reasons to justify such—" A gesture, faintly supercilious, indicated that a polite word could not be found for the enormity, the vulgarity, the unconscionable arrogance, the. . . . "Though I cannot imagine," she said, "exactly *what*. . . ."

150

"Hmm." He was smiling slightly and looking thoughtful. He had watched them play this game with one another in court, psychoanalytic experts on opposing sides responding to lawyers and to each other. They were consummate actors. He had learned a lot from them. He'd picked up a hobby from them, in fact; he'd picked up Freud and Jung, fathers of this one-upmanship game. Of course, he'd picked up the habit of reading in the seminary and never shed it. Pascal and Augustine still lay on his bedside table. But he'd added all sorts of things, and Freud and Jung were near the head of the list because they'd become part of the legal game. These days, there were brilliant psychopaths in prisons who could quote you chapter and verse on Freud. Any criminal lawyer worth his salt could throw around Freud these days. So Jake had taken up reading the biographers' accounts. Reading the letters. Reading about the piques, the rivalries, the metaphorical stabbing of dissenters. When it came down to it, he thought, who could be more defensive than the originator of the term "defensive"? Answer: possibly some of his disciples, the orthodox upholders of the tradition.

The most important lesson he'd picked up from their courtroom performances was the power of *waiting*.

"Sergeant Murphy," she said, with increased asperity. "If this is a purely frivolous—" The tented fingertips were now pressed rather tightly against each other, so that the cushioned edges turned from pink to white.

"No," he said. "Oh no, believe me. This is not a frivolous visit. Not at all. It's about homicide, Dr. Wilson."

She blinked rapidly a couple of times, but otherwise did not move.

He waited.

He saw the way her lips tightened, holding back the anger. She adjusted her ring again, then resumed the tented-hands position, the tips of the middle fingers just grazing the underside of her chin. "If you're after files on one of my patients, sergeant, you are surely well aware that that's privileged information. Not even a subpoena—"

"No, no," he said, brushing this aside. "That's not at all the kind of information I want." He smiled at her. "Actually, I'm already getting the kind I want."

She stood abruptly, knocking a large ring binder to the floor, her anger tripping over itself on her tongue. "You are sargeing—you are pluh—you are playing games with me, sergeant."

He crossed his right knee over his left and moved comfortably in his seat. "Doesn't that make two of us?" he asked.

She sat down again, breathing slowly. "Sergeant Murphy." She spoke patiently, as to a child. "I'm sure you believe you are doing your job. I'm sure that in your mind you have some valid reason for being here, and for behaving . . . rather childishly. Certainly rudely." The tented fingertips seemed slightly agitated now, beating time, drawing away from each other a half inch, coming back together, separating, trampoliners bouncing off each other. "What I don't think you understand is the importance of time to a professional therapist, the importance to other *lives*—"

"Ah, *lives*," he said. "Other *lives*. That's exactly what I'm interested in."

The tented fingers stilled. He detected a tremor at their tips. She said icily, "There's a certain form of behavior, sergeant, deviant behavior, that exhibits itself as an excessive need to *control*, although in actual fact it arises from extreme insecurity. We call it passive aggressive."

Ah, jargon. He'd had to swallow it by the bucketful for years. He'd watched it shuttlecocked around by experts, he'd listened to them juggling it, balancing it on the tips of their tongues, passing it behind their backs while tapping their tummies. Lovely plastic pliable all-purpose jargon. He beamed at her.

"Would you say—" he leaned forward, speaking softly, earnestly "—that you draw excessive pleasure, and a sense of self-worth, from controlling other lives?"

She recoiled as though punched. Before either of them could convert the idea of missile or trajectory into thought, a small black-plastic container, trailing paper clips, was zinging on a voyage toward his head. He ducked. Sounds of plastic cracking, and the soft tinkle of fifty pieces of wire skittering across the floor.

He smiled at her. "We call that aggressive," he said softly. "Plain and simple."

She was breathing heavily now. Breathing fire. He half expected to see flames leap from her mouth when she opened it.

"I'll get to the point," he said. "Which is game playing with other people's lives. Midnight phone calls, that sort of thing." He had to be careful now. Very careful. He was shooting in the dark. He knew the target was there, but if he shot and missed, he was in trouble. If he made a mistake, she would know he was guessing and would retreat. She was used to control, and knew how to behave when she had it. He had to keep her off balance. "We are talking about someone who was, we could almost say, courted by you as a patient. We are talking about Marni Verstak and her son." (Make her aware that I have privileged information. Make her wonder how much.) "We are talking about threatening phone calls in the middle of the night and a possible attempt to reinforce your patient's uncertainty about whether those phone calls actually occurred. I believe your professional association has rather harsh penalties for that sort of behavior from its members. Unethical's the politest word, isn't it?"

He could almost see the cogs whirring behind the tented and trembling hands. But she was very, very quick at recovering balance. Very quick. He thought: She senses I'm fishing for hard facts.

"Sergeant," she said with elaborate patience. "I do not expect you to understand the convoluted behaviors of the disturbed mind. Nor do I feel any need to justify treatment sanctioned by psychoanalytic literature and experience." The fingers bounced lightly against each other again, tentative trampoline artists. "However, I will say that I am used to the phenomenon of patients believing the therapist was somehow 'sent' to them, that the therapist singled them out, approached them. We are also, I can assure you, quite accustomed to the patient's hostility toward the therapist. We call this transference."

"Ah," he said. Jargon again, sweet jargon. He knew how to catch it and bounce it back. Conversationally he asked: "Curious, wasn't it, those two times Freud fainted in public?"

"What?" She blinked, disoriented.

"I've always wondered if. . . . But you're the expert, of course. Why do *you* think it happened?"

"I'm afraid I don't recall, off the top of my head. . . ."

He raised his eyebrows to indicate surprise that such a distinguished, et cetera. "Well, as I'm sure you remember, both times Jung was there. Both times Jung had just said something to him. Jung was politely disagreeing, of course." He waved the digression away. "But we were talking about midnight phone calls."

She said slowly, as though enunciating a textbook lesson, "The belief in malevolent anonymous phone calls in the middle of the night is a not-infrequent symptom of severe anxiety disorder. The patient projects inner fears onto the voice of the caller. The mind plays very elaborate tricks on us, sergeant. Particularly the mind of the disturbed person."

Disturbed. There it was again; again he felt an inner click.

"I see," he said. "This diagnosis, in the case of Ms. Verstak, would be based on the fact that there is no corroborating evidence for the calls?"

"Partly. Yes."

"The problem is," he said, "we *do* have corroborating evidence. Police evidence. We listened in on one of the calls."

"Oh." It took her several seconds of adjusting papers on her desk to recover. "Well, no therapist is infallible, of course. Though this does not alter—"

"Furthermore," he said, "we have evidence linking the caller to a number of fashionable addresses in the Back Bay, Copley Square." Careful, now. Careful. Don't blunder into a trip switch. You don't *know* she knows the caller, your radar is definitely picking up signals, but you could have the translation wrong. "He has very respectable contacts," he said. "Quite a roster. Even doctors' offices." Cunning generalizations, but unnerving if they hit home. Keep her wondering how much I know.

She was looking at him blandly, her fingers still. "I'm afraid I don't quite see what this has to—"

"We also have evidence linking him to the street in Jamaica Plain where Ms. Verstak has been restoring a house, and where a homicide occurred. We have evidence linking him to a drug-trafficking ring operating out of that street."

Her reaction surprised both of them. Eyes very wide with shock, the fingers interlaced now, the hands clasping each other, clenched. "But that's impos—That's ridiculous!"

He had to step carefully, carefully. So she knew the caller all right, but didn't know too much about him. "This would mean," he said deliberately, "that anyone found to have been involved with these threatening phone calls could be an accessory before the fact to a murder."

She turned pale. She got up and walked to her window and looked out. She came back and sat at her desk. She adjusted the pens on her desk, lining them up carefully and with great concentration, all the tips facing one way, level with the edge of her desk calendar. Then she became very still, and when she looked up again her eyes seemed to him curiously glazed, as though she were in a mild trance. When she spoke, it was as though the past few minutes had not occurred; it was as though she were continuing to instruct a rather dense layman in the higher mysteries of psychoanalytic method. Her eyes settled on him briefly, then wandered to a corner of her desk.

"If what you are saying is true, this is of course very shocking to me. Very distressing. Sometimes, you see, the members of our profession find themselves inadvertently at the mercy of . . . what you might call therapeutic technicians, persons of, ah, lower . . . persons on whom we rely for some aspects of treatment. I can assure you a full report will be made to the proper authorities if any irregularities. . . ."

All his senses were on full alert. It was not just that she was lying wildly and blindly. It was more complex, more interesting. She knew he knew she was lying.

"Sometimes an analyst has to take exceptional measures." She took a deep breath. He watched the elbows on the desk, the fingers tented again, bouncing lightly, just in front of the lips now. Obscuring the lips. So that she was speaking through the tunnel of her fingers. Her lashes brushed her cheek. She looked down along her fingers, concentrating. "Sometimes a form of shock treatment is indicated. Without going into details of confidential case history, Ms. Verstak came to me in some distress because of a love relationship gone wrong. The usual thing: she got involved with a married man and misinterpreted the nature of his interest. Her absorption in herself was so total—a common symptom of the disordered personality—that she was blind to the havoc she was causing in other peoples' lives."

Now the tented fingers went higher, the head lower, so that the bridge of her nose was lightly resting on the tips of her fingers. She looked like a woman at prayer. This is quite a performance, he thought.

"Havoc in other peoples' lives?" he repeated politely, the nuances carefully neutral.

She looked briefly up at him, and away again.

"Yes," she said. "Disturbed people are ferociously egocentric. What she was really looking for was a father substitute for her illegitimate child. What she was doing was wrecking someone else's marriage. Avoiding responsibility for her own actions. The telephone calls were the . . . shock treatment. Very carefully monitored, in fact. I had only the highest professional intentions." She looked at him now, her eyes glittering strangely. "The highest."

"I see." He was beginning to feel very uneasy. He was used to glibness, the way absolute certainty clashed with absolute (but contradictory) certainty in court, with neither side budging. The god itch, he called it. But he was not used to the passionately smooth justification of criminal activity. He had not expected that. She was giving off the same intensity as a trapped animal about to turn vicious.

She looked directly at him now, the inverted vee of her hands across her mouth. "If somehow inadvertent harm came. . . . But I simply don't understand, I don't see how. . . . The thing is, when we use, ah, unorthodox methods, we don't always know very much about the, ah, agents who, ah, carry out the prescribed source of treatment."

He thought: She's either crazy, or very very scared. Or both.

"Couple of things," he said, "I'm afraid I don't understand. Like, ah, how threatening death to a woman's child is saving someone else's marriage."

She looked at him vaguely for so long that he thought she must not have registered his comment. Then she said in her formal voice: "It was important to jolt her mind off herself and off the man with whom she was involved."

He kept watching her. He stretched out in the chair, making himself at ease, his laced hands behind his head, his feet extended. "Funny, the things that come back to you," he said meditatively. "Read something in a magazine a while back. Some article about body language by a psychiatrist. He claimed that putting the hands together like this—" he mimicked her tented fingers. "He was a Freudian, by the way. He claimed it was a symbol of a temple, church, synagogue, you know. Whatever. And that when people did that, talked through their hands like that, it was a sign that they knew they were talking bullshit, but they were giving it a moral coating. You agree with that stuff?"

Again, he seemed to hit some hidden button.

She said ferociously: "That smug bitch needs to know what it feels like. Having someone smash up your world. Having no way to fight back."

In the dead silence that followed, she seemed to see her own words hanging in the air between them. Her eyes narrowed for a split second on the brink of utter humiliation, and then it was as though she decided to expunge the past minute. The words had not been spoken.

"Was it your marriage being smashed?" he asked.

"Pardon?" she said. As though this were a complete non sequitur. As though he were slightly mad.

"Was it your marriage?"

There was a long silence. He waited. When she raised her head, he could hardly believe he was looking at the same woman, her face was so haggard. "I have never been married, sergeant." She said it very calmly and quietly.

He thought: Dumb question on my part.

Of course, Marni would have known if Ainsley were Mrs. Michael Lavan. Marni had had a phone call from Mrs. Lavan. He'd lost the advantage. He knew Ainsley Wilson was somewhere square in the middle of all that. But where and how? She would sense he had nothing concrete and she would stop being frightened.

He made an attempt to regain momentum: "So," he said. "Two homicides so far, to which you may legally be an accessory. All part of the shock treatment, is it?"

He monitored the flinch, the fingers trembling. "When you're fighting absolute power," she said, "you have to. . . . You find yourself resorting to. . . . Williams was another of his casualties, but I don't trust Williams. With people like Williams," she said, "you lose all. . . . It's apparent that something else all together is going on, and I don't know what it is."

"Williams?" he said, thinking aloud. And then could have kicked himself. Damn. The caller, of course. Big Turk hadn't given him a name for Mr. Lisp.

She looked at him sharply, a sudden surge of relief in her eyes. "Ah, but I thought you knew all about Williams."

Damn, damn, damn. Caught out. But he did believe one part of her story, not the part in words. He believed in her panic. That was real. And he believed she had not intended the kind of harm that had been set in motion.

He remembered Marni's circles on the coffee table.

There were different circles. They just happened to be rolling in the same direction at the same time.

Williams was another of his casualties. . . .

Of whose casualties? But he wouldn't get anything more from her now. He'd lost the edge.

"Our investigations are proceeding in multiple directions," he said. "You do understand that you may eventually be charged with being an accessory to murder?"

He was not sure if she heard. There was no expression on her face.

"Is there anything else you wish to tell me?" he asked.

"It was like a madness, like a virus," she said, although he did not think she knew she had spoken the words aloud. She looked at him vaguely. But her eyes were somewhere else altogether. Whatever she was seeing, he did not expect any more answers.

It was almost noon when Jake Murphy got to his office, where a number of pieces of news reached him more or less simultaneously. He saw the morning tabloid lying open on the receptionist's counter as he went by, and he saw the picture of Marni with Alonso and Jacobson. Drugs, deaths, kickbacks in the city's real estate wars, he read. He saw the picture of Michael Lavan; the picture of Roger.

"What the hell?" he said, grabbing it and taking it into his office. He was skimming the page when the pink phone-memo slips on his spike file caught his eye. He scooped them off. Marni had tried to reach him several times. Also Leon, the street kid from Jamaica Plain, had called, but would not leave a message, a last name, or a number.

He dialed Marni's office number and was letting it ring for a sixth time when Pete Barber, head of homicide, came in, indicating urgency. Jake hung up. He heard about the Beacon Street murder. He heard about the arrest.

"Jesus, Pete," he said. "Where is she?"

He heard that formal charges had already been laid.

"Gonna have egg on your face, Pete," Jake fumed. "Why the hell didn't you check with me first?"

"Maybe I would've if you checked in here once in a while, you goddamn loner. Except I don't see what the hell it's got to do with you."

"It's got everything," Jake shouted. "The Jamaica Plain stabbing, that turnpike crash, this. It's all the same thing, it's a drug scam."

"Jake, I already had a complaint from the DEA, they think you're off your—"

"Yeah, maybe. And maybe we'll have more homicides if we don't—" He was grabbing handfuls of his hair with frustration. "Look, Pete, I haven't got time to. . . . Just trust me. I got to. . . ." He grabbed his coat and was leaving the room when the phone rang. He swore, hesitated, wrenched the receiver from its cradle.

"That Sergeant Murphy?"

"Yes."

"Leon here. You see the *Sun* this morning, sarge? There's a picture of a dude on page two. Lavan, it says under. That's the dude, sarge. The one that drove the fancy car when those guys come onto our turf."

"Holy shit," Jake said. He was caught between a frantic desire to get to Marni, and an urge to follow up the first piece of hard evidence he had. "You sure, Leon?"

"Pos-i-*tive*."

"Can you get yourself down here? Make an ID for us? I'll make it worth your while."

"Okay," Leon said.

"Pete," Jake said. "There's a real-estate lawyer, Michael Lavan, same company as Verstak, same office. Bring him in. Drugs, accessory to homicide. I've got a witness coming." He grabbed his coat, headed for his car and Marni. But the warden told him that bail had already been paid, she'd been taken home, so he headed toward Mt. Vernon Street, fuming at the crawling traffic.

17: Geraint the Comforter

Back inside her apartment, Marni felt safer. More normal. Able to think again. And the preeminent thought was this: Matthew was lying safely in a hospital bed, watched over by an undercover policeman. That was the main thing.

"It's so kind of you," she said to Geraint. It was comforting to have him there. "Can I fix you coffee?" For no reason, the image of Anderson looking at the photographs of Matthew interposed itself, and she put her hands over her face. "Oh poor Andy," she said, and the word turned into a sob. "Poor Andy. It's so horrible. I can't. . . . I can't *believe* it."

"What a gentle soul you are," Geraint said tenderly. He took her in his arms and stroked her hair and kissed her on the forehead, a brotherly and chaste sort of kiss.

Geraint did care about him, she thought. He did love him in his own way. She felt a surge of affection for him, and let herself cry on his shoulder. "Poor Andy," she wept. She remembered something and raised her head suddenly. "Gerry, you didn't tell me he had. . . . You didn't tell me he was dying. I was stunned when I saw him."

"He didn't want anyone to know," Geraint said. "He wanted me to spirit him out of the country before Abigail had any inkling."

She extricated herself from his embrace and went to the kitchen, fussing with the coffee maker. "Abigail," she said neutrally.

"Yes." He grimaced. "Dreadful woman."

She made some sound of agreement. She registered that his almost cast had made a reappearance, the sort of thing Abigail did to people's

161

nerves. Marni didn't have the energy to think about Abigail. Her mind slid to Andy. "He looked so frail. So thin."

"That's why I didn't want him upset," Geraint said. "You know how he frets needlessly about that sort of thing. Thought you understood that, Marni."

She frowned. "What sort of thing?" What she felt was a sudden shiver of caution, of bewilderment. He was doing it again. Talking as though he knew about Matthew. (Though God knows, all of Boston could know about him now, once a wardful of nurses knew.) She watched him carefully, her heart unaccountably fluttering, waiting for clues, feeling as though she were stranded in a mine field, not wanting to put a foot down wrong.

Geraint said smoothly: "I know. You thought you were protecting him. But he prefers not to know names, you see, and in any case she was a non-issue. A non-affair. Whatever she may have told you, my dear, is sour grapes, I'm afraid. Hell hath no fury, et cetera. I think she may well be in cahoots with Abigail and behind this whole thing."

Marni felt pins and needles in the crannies of her mind. She thought several things simultaneously: he's not talking about Matthew; I don't know what he's talking about; he's anxious about something; he thinks I know something I don't. What is it? Marking time, fishing for clues, she said: "You think Abigail and she. . .?"

"Oh God yes," he said lightly, one eye wandering markedly out of focus. "They both cast a wide net. You can be sure either Abigail tracked down Ainsley, or vice versa."

"*Ainsley?*" she said involuntarily. Astonished. "You know Ainsley?"

It was Geraint's turn to look momentarily surprised. He seemed to assimilate several pieces of information at once from her statement. She could see translations flickering across his irises. He laughed. "Oh," he said. "Well, well. A prime mover outmaneuvered. Ainsley played her cards well. An intelligent woman," he said, smiling to himself. "But then, that's what attracts me."

Marni felt the way she always felt with Geraint. Completely at sea. Uneasy. Nervous. She noticed that his eyes were now in crisp and proper alignment.

She said carefully: "I never realized you and Ainsley. . . ."

"No. Well, there you are," he said with a charming smile. "It was a meaningless thing, so there was no sense at all in getting Andy distressed. And when I knew she'd approached you, I naturally thought this was her way to, you know. . . . A woman scorned. That sort of thing."

In Marni's mind, there was something just the other side of a haze. But to reach it, she had to look at the idea of Andy murdered, and her mind veered away from this. She had the sense of herself in a hallway with her hands over her ears.

". . . on the grapevine," Geraint was saying. "Perhaps you should tell me all about it?"

"What? Sorry, I wasn't—"

"Anderson's putative son. A different kettle of fish entirely. If it's true, it was churlish of you not to tell him. I think he would have been delighted, as a matter of fact."

So he *did* know. "I thought that's what you were talking about all along," she said. "I thought that's what you meant."

"Ah," he said. "Crossed wires everywhere we turn. Of course, how Abigail will react is another matter. And if *I've* heard on the grapevine, Abigail has heard. If I were you, I would be very, very nervous."

Marni's hands shook a little as she took mugs from the cupboard, poured coffee. Geraint was watching her.

"Abigail's ruthless," he said.

She handed him a mug of coffee. She could feel her heart booming like a drum.

"As a matter of fact," he said. "I suspect her of killing Andy."

She lurched, and a wave of coffee leaped from her mug to the floor.

"To keep things quiet, you know," he said. "Before anyone knew he had AIDS. A sacrificial lamb to the fierce god of Back Bay respectability, Brahmin honor, and all that. Marni, you're spilling coffee at a great rate there."

"What? Oh." Automatically, she picked up a dishcloth and mopped at the stain on the carpet.

"Oh, I know Andy thinks she knew nothing about it," he said. "Or so he tried to convince himself." He laughed shortly. "But there isn't anything Abigail doesn't know."

Marni mopped at her carpet, but the walls of Andy's hallway were closing in on her. The haze. There was something it was imperative to know. A spilled tray. Yes. It came back to her now.

Williams at the door. The voice of Williams. She shuddered. And then Andy's voice: "Geraint found him for me."

She felt suddenly very frightened.

"Of course," Geraint said smoothly. "I don't mean that I think she literally did it herself. She would have used that awful housekeeper Williams, who was one of her spies."

Marni felt her heart thumping like a brass drum. It was dangerous to have a thought. Geraint could see thoughts.

"I could barely stay one step ahead of her," Geraint said. "I'd find servants Andy could trust, and the next thing I knew they were double agents. I had to get rid of them like dominoes. Poor Andy was a wreck. She'll stop at nothing, that woman."

"Gerry," she said. She wanted rather urgently to be alone, all the locks and chains on the door, the windows bolted, the blinds drawn, the lights on, the stereo filling the air with Mozart. "I think I have to, you know. . . . So much has happened, I guess it's shock, but I simply have to sleep."

"Well, of course," he said gallantly. "You know, Marni, I happen to know that Andy has left you a generous stipend. You should think about a nice safe place outside Boston, leave this real-estate business, the inner city. You won't need it any more. It's a dangerous game, you know." He bent over and took her chin in his hand. "Very dangerous."

She thought: Is he threatening me?

"You're such a fragile little thing," he said. He ran an index finger along her eyebrows, down her nose, around her lips. Lightly. An erotic invitation that felt sinister. "I'd like to do another series of photographs. Serious ones, a hymn to the body, you know the kind of thing I mean. We'll take a week or so, shall we? I'd like to find you somewhere safe. The Maine coast, perhaps? For you and the little boy when he gets out of the hospital."

Marni swallowed. Is this just about sex? she wondered. Or something more? This was not a game of strength. Or of wills. It was a game of IQs. Two could play this game, even if one of them was frightened. One thing Marni knew for certain: Geraint was only interested in a woman (in anyone) if she (or he) had not yet capitulated. Object: don't get him angry, but keep him on the line.

She removed his hand from her chin, but pressed her lips against his fingers. "You're like a brother to me, Gerry. I'm very grateful." Demurely flirtatious, eyes contradicting the words. "Something Andy said to me, you know over dinner. . . ." Her voice broke. "In the crunch, he said, you didn't violate a trust. And I do know he's right, deep down, even if I haven't always, well, fully trusted you."

She saw the quick glitter in his eyes: the pleasure of the chase; the belief that he had her where he wanted her.

"Well, then," he said. "We'll arrange something. When's the little boy coming out of hospital?"

Her buzzer went and she answered it gratefully.

"Sergeant Murphy," the speaker said in a fuzz of static. "Can I come up?"

Jake! She was weak with relief. "Come right in, sergeant," she said, trying to keep her voice neutral, pressing the lock release buttons.

"Well, I'll be off then." Geraint gave her a kiss on the forehead.

"Oh, please don't go," she said politely. "It's so demoralizing to have the police—"

But he was not to be caught.

"Marni," he said. "You can wind any policeman around your little finger. And you don't have a thing to worry about. I'll have to make a visit to the Dragon Lady, see about funeral arrangements. I'll let you know what I find out."

He went down the staircase while Jake rose through the solitary and ancient elevator shaft.

And then Jake was there. In her apartment. She locked all the locks and then turned.

"Jake," she whispered. She had never felt so happy to see anyone in her life. She wanted to tell him a million things, but all she did was sob and sob and sob in his arms.

"It's all right," he said. "It's all right. Everything will be okay, the net's closing in now."

He was on official business. He hadn't intended anything other than. . . . And by now they should have Michael Lavan at the precinct office, he had to go. But certain kinds of momentum cannot be resisted, there are certain forces of nature, earthquakes, hurricanes, passion, and the like. . . .

Anyway. It wasn't as though either of them made a decision. Or didn't make a decision. It just happened. It was like a fabulous tornado. A pleasurable cataclysm. They made strange noises, sometimes sounds like laughter, sometimes almost like sobbing. And afterwards they lay very silently together on her bed. The bed with the blue floral sheets.

He thought: I mustn't presume that this means anything in the long run. People behave one way in crisis, another way after. You can't assume anything.

She thought: I was ravenous. For sex and safety, both. I can hardly tell one from the other. But I don't know what I feel. I don't want to feel anything. I don't ever want to feel anything at all, never again, ever. Except for Matthew, that's different. With a child, you don't even have a choice.

"I have to get back to the office," Jake said.

They were as gentle and courteous to each other as strangers as they dressed, delicately looking away, standing back to back as they pulled on clothes.

"I'll call you from my office," he said.

"Yes." She hadn't even told him about. . . . "Oh God," she said in a panic. "All the things I have to tell you." Words came in a jumble: Abigail, Geraint, Williams, the photographs.

"Slow down," he said. "It's all right. Everything's all right. One at a time, there's no rush. I'm not leaving till you've told me everything."

"There was a horrible man at Andy's, his housekeeper. Williams."

"Williams!"

"Yes. I heard him speak. He's Mr. Lisp, the man who made the calls. He must have killed Andy."

In the act of tucking shirt into pants, Jake stopped, electrified. "Williams was *there*? God."

He began dialing his office, stopped and dialed his contact number for Big Turk instead, but got no answer. Quadratic equations were popping inside his head with the speed of lightning.

Ainsley Wilson—Mr. Lisp—Marni.

Michael Lavan—Jamaica Plain—Joseph Lucyk—Marni.

Mr. Lisp—Anderson Thorpe—Marni.

Okay, but what was the x factor? Who?

"Andy said Geraint got Williams for him. But Geraint thinks Abigail's behind it. And—"

"Abigail. Geraint," Jake said. How did all this fit? His shirt was half buttoned, he had on one sock; the other he'd absentmindedly tucked into his shirt pocket. He forgot about dressing and paced, knuckles pressed against his cheekbone, just below the eyes. "Keep talking," he said tersely. "Anything you can think of."

Any detail might do it. Trip the switch.

"Um," she said. "Well, Geraint knows about Matthew, I don't know how, I suppose from the hospital somehow. And, um, he thinks Williams was a spy for Abigail. And he even thinks Abigail and Ainsley. . . ."

She stopped abruptly. They looked at each other, hearing sirens.

"God, how could I forget to tell you that? He knows Ainsley," she said. "He's had an affair with Ainsley." She concentrated, pressing her fingertips to her eyelids. "But wait, there's something. There are other circles. Circles inside circles. He was afraid Ainsley had told me something, he was afraid I was going to tell Andy. He didn't realize I didn't know about him and Ainsley."

Jake paced, thinking. *Williams is another of his casualties,* Ainsley Wilson had said.

"You think it ended badly?" he asked. "His affair with Ainsley?"

"All Geraint's affairs end badly. For the other person." She waved her hands, searching for a way to explain. "He turns people into . . . he *destroys* them."

Jake paced, one sock on, one off. "Williams made the phone calls, and Wilson fed him information to use."

Of course, Marni thought. *She* knew about Matthew. I think I'd even told her—yes, I'd mentioned my floral sheets, describing that last breakfast in bed with Michael.

"But Geraint Finnbar must be the missing link," Jake mused. "I've got to get something concrete. . . . And Lavan in that car in Jamaica Plain. . . ."

"Oh," she said. "Speaking of Michael. I got fired, by the way. Or as good as." It seemed an oddly esoteric and irrelevant piece of information. "There was unbelievable stuff in the paper. Then Michael told Roger that I'm the leak to Olde Pilgrim."

Jake rolled his eyes. "There's a warrant out for his arrest."

"For Michael's?"

"In it up to his ears."

I want to go very far away with Matthew, she thought. A place like Wilderness, Vermont. Only farther away, and safer.

"Look," Jake said, seeing a tremor in her hands. "I'm not sure that your son has anything to do with this, except accidentally. But in any case, he's under guard. It's you I'm worried about. I'm calling for someone to watch this place. Don't leave your apartment until I call you, okay?"

He called the precinct office, arranged for a watch on Marni's place. He heard that Michael Lavan had not been at his law office, or the real-estate office, or his home. His wife said he'd gone on a business trip. An APB was put out, giving the lawyer's description.

Jake stayed until he saw the two cars he was waiting for: one parked in Louisberg Square, watching the front door; another in Acorn Street watching the fire escape.

"Okay," he said. "You're safe. The place is under surveillance."

"Thank you, Jake." She put a hand up to his cheek, just for a second. She felt ridiculously shy again. I have just made love to this man, she thought with amazement.

I don't want to assume anything, Jake thought. I don't want to startle her off, make her regret it.

They stood there awkwardly, looking at each other, as nervous as two high-school kids on a first date. They parted almost formally, just touching hands lightly.

He couldn't wait for the elderly elevator. He ran down four flights of stairs.

He needed street evidence on Lavan, Williams, Finnbar.

He needed Big Turk.

18: Mr. Lisp

If he sat in the diner under the subway tracks in Jamaica Plain and ate enough doughnuts, the network would do the trick. Jake could scarcely begin to imagine the intricacies of this network. All he knew was the word would get to Big Turk. He didn't want to know what Big Turk passed him off as, but you could bet he wasn't known as a cop.

Rephrase that. He *hoped* he could bet that no one knew him as a cop. Not here.

Damn. If he drank any more coffee, he'd be awake till next fall, though it would probably be worth it. Give Big Turk an assignment, and he'd dig up so much dirt you needed a dump truck to take it off and sift through it.

Hearty thump on the shoulder. "Got something for you, my man." Big Turk slid into his alcove. "Pretty pictures. They cost me, they gonna cost you." He pulled a Manila envelope from under his parka.

"How much?"

"Twice whatever you're thinking. I owe some very steep favors for these. You're gonna think six birthdays come at once. Pickies of your Mr. Lisp and some very notable people without their clothes on."

"How much?"

Big Turk peeked into the envelope, counting. "Twenty eight-by-ten glossies in full black-and-white technidrama. Hundred bucks each, it's a steal."

"Shit," Jake said. "All right. Done. I'll get it to you."

Big Turk smiled, waiting.

170

"Well, I don't exactly carry that around in ready cash," Jake said.

Big Turk laughed and tapped his forehead. "Must be getting soft in the head." But he handed over the envelope.

The usual sleazy stuff. Well, not quite. This was sleaze with pretensions. Arty. Somewhere between erotica and soft porn. Women tied to pieces of abstract sculpture, lashed over rain barrels, sometimes the point of a switchblade touching a nipple like a feather, sometimes a bird's beak; sometimes knives between their legs, sometimes wetter and more pliable objects. Also men tied up, men wrestling, men being whipped. And then the classy, arty touches: a cat licking breasts, a dog gnawing a vagina, a man lying in the middle of a dinner table that was elegantly set with crystal and silverware, a large nutcracker being closed around his testicles by a butler in black tie and cutaway. Jake recognized the man on the table, a politician.

"Christ," he said softly. "That one must be good for payola with residuals."

The way light and shadow were used in the photographs made you think of an art gallery. But the faces would give you nightmares. They were abject. Without hope. There was nothing at all in their eyes; they were as blank as the eyes of the blind. Jake felt his stomach turn. In all the photographs, the same man was holding the knives, the leash of the dog, the nutcracker.

"That's Williams?"

"That's Williams. Scum of the earth, smaller than a flea. Slave work, petty blackmail."

"Murder when asked?"

"Maybe. Nothing violent. He's wimp to the core."

Of the other faces in the photographs, Jake recognized a local news anchorwoman, a judge, a few women who looked vaguely familiar from the society pages of the newspapers. And Ainsley.

"Oh Jesus," he said, looking away. He wished he'd been kinder to her that morning.

"S'matter with you?" Big Turk said. "You abnormal or something? There's more of that chick. Keep going. Very interesting stuff."

In the next, there were two women in chains and Williams in boots and with a whip. The two women looked alike.

"Sisters," Big Turk said. "But here's the really interesting part. This one is your Dr. Wilson. This other one, the older sister, is the wife of your lawyer guy. This is Mrs. Michael Lavan."

Okay. Now he had his case. "You know who took these?"

"Yeah," Big Turk said. "You'll never nail him. Floats above it all, way above, it's all fun and games and art to him. Never gets a speck of dust under his fingernails. You try to nail him, you in bigger trouble if you win than if you lose."

"Yeah, well. That's my problem, not yours."

"Blackmail's nothing, man. Pin money for Williams, blackmail's the nice side of the business. Stick with the little fellas, get Williams, give yourself a pat on the back. And let Lavan slip through your fingers, know what I mean? Because the man behind the camera is not gonna risk Lavan talking. Man behind the camera's out of your league."

"Listen," Jake said. "I know who took the photographs, don't waste my time. Just tell me what else you've got on him."

"You know who took the pics?"

"Yeah, I know."

"You want the saint-of-the-year award, right? Candles and incense and all that shit? Shrine when you're gone?" Big Turk shook his head in disbelief. "Okay. Your funeral. Not that you'll be able to do anything with it. For starters, the word is he's been milking Thorpe and a raft of other filthy-rich dummies for years. Start-up and maintenance capital for his drug empire. Brings the stuff in with art shipments, sculptures from Mexico, Colombia, that sort of thing. Gets it out through a real-estate network, art dealerships, little street flunkies, a hundred ways. Investment broker for a lot of very respectable money. People give him, they get a tax-free windfall every month, they don't ask questions. Give enough to the right political campaigns, the right causes, who's gonna complain? You start messing with his retail area, like your little lady friend in real estate, you wind up in big trouble. You start messing with his investment business, you wind up in bigger trouble. Make a lot of powerful people very nervous."

Jake tapped the pictures of Ainsley. "She'll testify. I'll pressure Williams and Lavan, plea bargaining, they'll testify. The DEA is riding high, the First Lady's saying no to drugs, we'll nail him."

"Who you kidding? Rash of accidents before you ever get near a court. Car crashes. Muggings. A whole lotta chance gonna happen, man."

"You ever heard of protective custody?"

"You ever heard of radioactive? Man, you gonna give off so much trouble, nobody touch you with a forty-foot pole."

"You know when an art shipment's coming in?"

"Man," Big Turk said. "Sometimes I think you gotta be a choirboy in disguise." He slid out from his seat, discussion over. "Whole lotta chance gonna happen," he warned again.

At Special Branch, Jake had photography make a fast reprint of one of the photographs, had them do a close-up and blow-up of Williams's face, had a flyer done. He signed an arrest warrant, which never even got to first base.

Sergeant Jimmy Gencarelli, en route to the dispatcher, took one look at the flyer.

"Uh, Jake," he said. "Found a stiff this morning answers to this description. Bench in Franklin Park, Jamaica Plain. Booze and exposure, looks like."

Whole lotta chance gonna happen.

Then Michael Lavan's body was found in his car in his own garage, windows closed, engine running.

Did Jake have a case left?

He had the photographs of Dr. Ainsley Wilson. He called her. There was a thirty-second wait, then the receptionist put him through.

"Dr. Wilson? Sergeant Murphy. I've got some pictures of you and your sister and Williams. Willing to keep them out of the press and the courts if you've got anything useful to tell me." There was a long silence. "Dr. Wilson?"

"Yes," she said in a low voice, and the silence continued. At last she said: "I don't expect you to believe me, but one of my motives was good. It was my only way to get back at him. He's the major beneficiary of Thorpe's will. I thought the odds were if Thorpe knew he had an heir, he'd change his will. I was trying to get her to tell

Thorpe. I expect she did, and that's why—"

Motive.

"Good," he said eagerly. "Anything else?"

"I won't testify in court, sergeant. Not even if you subpoena me. Not even if I face contempt."

"Noted. If you think of anything else, give me a call."

He called Marni. "Did you know that Finnbar's the beneficiary of your husband's will?"

"I always assumed that. Jake, I've had another call from Mr. Lisp."

"What?"

"He just said: 'Don't count on the hospital, my dear. First your son, then Murphy.' "

"But he's dead," Jake said. "Williams is dead."

"He can't be." *First your son.* . . . "Jake, I have to see Matthew!"

"All right. I'll tell my men. Take a cab from door to door."

"Um, Jake?"

"Mm?"

"Well, uh. . . . I was wondering. . . . I know you're frightfully busy."

Something warm moved through him like a flush of whiskey. "I have to go to the morgue first, check on this corpse that's supposed to be Williams. Then I'll join you at the hospital."

Then he'd need to take her to the morgue, in fact. Was the body, or was it not, Williams? She could give a definite answer. But he didn't want to saddle her with a gloomy task at the moment. "I'll be there as soon as I can," he said. "Don't leave till I join you."

19: The Dungeon Master

"But Mrs. Verstak," the nurse said, surprised. "The grandparents came for the children this morning, and your brother was with them. They were all discharged."

"My brother?"

"Yes. He said that on account of all the, uh—" the nurse looked away, embarrassed "—publicity, you didn't want to come here yourself. He said you'd asked him—"

"But the surveillance? The police surveillance?"

"Well, the grandparents. . . . The police have seen them every day, they knew them."

"Yes," Marni said. "Thank you."

White-faced, she went to the pay phone down the hall and called Steve's parents in Wellesley. "Oh Marni," Steve's mother said. "Yes, Steve's nice friend Geraint called us and picked us up. Such a lovely man. He drove us home with the children, I thought you knew. He said he was meeting you in Vermont, he's got little Matthew with him. We said, feel free to stay at the farm for a few days, dear."

Marni felt the super calm that settled on her in moments of crisis. She stood for one minute in the door of Eva's room and watched. No change, the nurse said. It was a coma. Eva might have been the Sleeping Beauty, suspended, waiting for the magical overthrow of evil.

Marni called Jake's office. It was terribly urgent, could they reach him at the morgue and tell him to call the hospital? Please, it was urgent. She paced the corridor near the reception desk. Five minutes, ten minutes, she couldn't stand it. She thought of asking the surveillance cars to take her to Vermont, but dismissed this idea instantly. One: they probably wouldn't do it until they got approval, by which time it might be too late. And two: Geraint would never let himself be corraled by a squad of police cars. She had to stalk him on her own. She had to get to him before he harmed Matthew. She called Special Task Force again. Tell Sergeant Murphy she'd gone to Wilderness, Vermont, to get her son. She left the number of Steve's parents; tell Sergeant Murphy to call this number for additional information.

From a window she could see the surveillance cars. She left by a door that went into the back parking lot. Her car was still in the Exeter Street garage. She took a cab there, got her car, took the turnpike west.

On the two-and-half-hour drive, thoughts must have come and gone at a dazzling rate through Marni's mind, but she was not conscious of thinking about anything. She was not conscious of time or distance. She kept an image of Matthew in the forefront of her vision like a beacon. All she knew, along every synapse and nerve end, was that she would find him, that he would be safe, that she would bring him home to live with her, that no other possibility would be allowed.

It seemed a matter of minutes from when she drove out of the Exeter Street garage till she turned into the rutted, snow-covered, winding drive leading to the farm.

She could see smoke rising from the chimney.

She braked with ferocity, churning snow. She was on the porch, hurling open the door, ready for—

"Mommy!" Matthew called. "Me and Uncle Gerry are playing I Spy."

Her son was in a rocker in front of a roaring fire, a blanket pulled up to his waist, not quite covering the cast.

"Oh Matt, mommy missed you." She was hugging him, laughing, crying.

Geraint sat in another rocker, smoking his pipe. Matthew seemed unperturbed. It was as though she had burst in on a scene of utmost domestic tranquillity.

"Marni," Geraint said, for all the world like an indulgent uncle or older brother. "We've been waiting for you. Would you like some Brie and sherry? Or I could make you a hot rum toddy if you'd prefer. Beastly cold outside."

She picked Matthew up, sat in the rocker, and held him on her lap. Geraint brought a tray containing cheese and crackers, a flask of sherry, a crystal glass. She stared at him in disbelief.

"Oh, my dear," he laughed. "It's not what I gave Andy, or Williams, if that's what you're thinking. Those were different situations altogether." He placed the tray on a small table beside her chair, poured himself some sherry and drank a mouthful. He cut a slice of Brie and ate it. "You see? Perfectly safe. You'll have a little?" One eye was focused on her; the other not quite.

"No, thank you."

"As you wish." Geraint shrugged and went back to his rocker.

"Williams is dead?" she asked in a flat voice.

"Completely, I'm afraid. He'd become a complication."

She pressed her lips together. "How long ago did he . . .?"

Geraint laughed. "Oh, the phone call," he said. "Confusing for you, isn't it?" He mimicked Williams's voice to perfection, right down to the lateral lisp: *"First your son, then Murphy."* He laughed again. "I play a lot of roles, my dear."

She faced him across a braided rug, hugging Matthew tightly. The child seemed drowsy, now, his head on her shoulder. "I have no idea how to talk to you," she said. "You're like someone from another planet. Why did you do this?" But the only possible answer flew into her mind like a black bat. *Psychopath.* There was no other explanation.

He raised his eyebrows. Such a quirky question, he implied, smiling urbanely. "I thought it was the best place to talk without interruption. Would you have preferred somewhere else?"

A line from *Hamlet*, not looked at since freshman year in college, rose into her mind like a tiny bubble rising through water: *. . . that one may smile, and smile, and be a villain.* And a child may sleep through villainy, she thought amazed, stroking Matthew's hair, rocking, rocking.

"You've been quite an irritant in the last little while, my dear," he sighed. "Of course, I'm very partial to fillies with spirit, they make by far the best racehorses. But you've certainly caught me off guard." He shook his head with amazement. "To think that neither Steven, that *irritatingly* naive flower child, nor the intensely neurotic and vengeful Dr. Wilson, nor even, for a while, the two-timing Williams, not one of them spilled the beans to me about your son. Astonishing, really. I must be losing my touch.

"Until Williams got a gut sense that covert rebellion would get him nowhere. So he called me, and when I arrived there was poor, silly Andy writing holograph alterations to his will. Touchingly sentimental, don't you think?"

There will be nothing to appeal to, Marni was thinking. No sense of honor, decency, shame, human feeling. Nothing. None of these apply.

Wait: there was one thing. Vanity. Especially intellectual and esthetic vanity. That was Geraint's Achilles' heel.

"Was Andy really reading Lowell's *Life Studies*, Gerry? Or was that your touch?" she asked.

"Marni, my dear." He was clearly delighted. "You recognized my ironic signature. What a clever little woman you are."

"One thing puzzles me," she said. "I didn't think you were indifferent to Andy's devotion—"

"Indeed not. It endeared him to me from the start, in that horrid school. It formed my tastes, you might say."

"Well, there's my dilemma, Gerry." She raised an arch eyebrow, walking a fine line between pleasing him and angering him. "Since we both know you're the world's ultimate narcissist, I'm surprised you could bring yourself to, ah, tamper with his final image of you."

Geraint smiled across his sherry glass. "My dear, you underestimate me. Andy died blissfully content. It was humanitarian in every possible way. No pain, no long-drawn-out wasting away, no ignominy. I tucked him in and brought him Lowell and sherry. I kissed him good night on the forehead. Really, it was so touching, it almost brought tears to my eyes." He took out a silk handkerchief and made a theatrical gesture of grief, half mocking, half serious. "It was a far, far better thing that I did. . . . Et cetera. He died knowing he had a son, he died believing I'd see everything was taken care of (as *indeed*, indeed I will), he died believing Abigail would never know the oh-so-uninteresting truth. And in fact, I don't think the Dragon Lady does, though one can never be certain. She's a tough old bird."

"I don't understand how the . . . I mean, the lesions and so on. It was obvious he had AIDS. How come there was nothing in the paper, and not even in the police report? Because Jake saw. . . ."

"My dear," Geraint said. "I have certain people in the police force in the palm of my hand. It was another of my little kindnesses. If Abigail knows, she doesn't know it because of me."

"This morning, you said *she* was behind—"

"Yes, well, I was still in the dark on one or two details, wasn't I? I didn't want you leaping to the right conclusions before I was ready. But the Dragon Lady had nothing to do with Andy's fond farewell, which I had to arrange rather hastily. I think I did a very creditable job on short notice, don't you?"

"Do you know, even when you paid my bail it never entered my head that you would actually. . . . I thought Williams did it."

"Good God," he said, offended. "That *driven* little man! You thought him capable of such finesse?"

"I suppose you could say his phone calls had finesse. Of a grotesque sort."

"The phone calls," Geraint said, tapping his forehead with his manicured fingernails. "Dear me. There again, you see, little flourishes going on quite without my knowledge. Quite without my permission." He wagged a schoolmasterish finger. "And Williams, a little flea like Williams, not even telling me until the end. Very naughty indeed. We shall definitely have to think up an appropriate punishment for Ainsley, won't we? Something much more refined than I gave Williams. I always try to make the punishment fit the crime."

Marni began to feel as though she were Alice in Wonderland trying to talk to the White Rabbit, or to the Queen who screamed *Off with her head!* A sort of giddiness came over her, a sense of time out. Since the conversation was completely and dangerously mad, yet strangely calm, and with such a weird surface of rationality, she had the sense that she could—as it were—get away with murder in conversation.

"Gerry," she said. "Were you always like this? From the start? Or did something . . .?"

"Was I always like what, my dear?"

"Without any discernible moral sense."

He threw back his head and laughed. "Actually," he said, quite earnestly and thoughtfully, "the term for my condition is severe dissociation. Put bluntly: there's an uncrossable abyss between thought and feeling. In a nutshell: I don't *feel*. I don't know what a feeling is, except by observation. And sometimes I regret the lack, you know. For example, I see you nuzzling your son's hair like that. Very pretty. It must be . . . *interesting* to have the sense of that current going back and forth between you and the child.

"Or take love." He sipped thoughtfully at his sherry. He might have been delivering a scholarly meditation. "I can see its power, the way it makes people—" he grimaced with mild contempt "—makes them *debase* themselves. And in literature, of course, the reverse, the ennobling thing. As with Desdemona, for example, in *Othello*. Though I can't say I've seen any of that side of love in real life. Still, it's theoretically possible. At least for most people, it's clearly a force. I rather regret not being able to experience that.

"On the other hand, a dissociative disorder puts me in the very first rank in history. Genghis Khan, Ivan the Terrible, Alexander the Great. Interesting, isn't it? I've read up on the phenomenon quite extensively. We're the subject of an endless stream of monographs and scholarly articles and art. We do seem to come to spectacularly bad ends, which should give the rest of you comfort.

"To be perfectly honest, I'm a bit of a junkie on the subject. I keep flirting with causes and cures, it's a little hobby. I'm a textbook case: slum kid in rich kids' school; regular sexual molestation by a teacher in the school." He turned his profile to her and fluttered his lashes. "The cost of personal beauty, I fear.

"As for cures, well, that's why a woman like Ainsley is briefly irresistible. Social workers, therapists, I can't resist them. But it never works. I run rings around them, I tie them in knots, the game becomes tedious very, very quickly."

He yawned elaborately.

"So there you are, my dear. Incorrigible. How did you put it? Without any discernible moral sense, almost right from the beginning." He laughed again, then leaned forward and spoke very earnestly. "But I suppose you could date some things from school. That's when I became an acute student of double standards and hypocrisies, especially among the wealthy and among the pillars of society. I like the way, for example, that certain people in the State Department bow and scrape because of certain contacts of mine. In Panama and Colombia, you know. And I do enjoy noting what people in very high office indeed will agree to, in return for a sizeable contribution to a campaign coffer. It's terribly interesting. In my own quite careless and indifferent way, I'm a moral scourge. I look for the weaknesses. I expose them. Merely for the fun of it, of course."

She was rocking back and forth, back and forth. Matthew was asleep in her arms, and she was swamped by a great, helpless wave of love for her son. She thought: imagine not being able to feel this.

Geraint's shadow fell across Matthew's body, and the muscle in her chest wall constricted. She still felt weirdly, unnaturally calm, but her mind raced. This was a dangerous game. A winner-keeps-all game. He didn't lure her here for philosophical discussion.

"Pretty," he said, looking down at them. "Very pretty. It pleases me esthetically, the idea of you with Andy's son. That's why I've decided to have you bear mine. For the symmetry." He laughed with delight. "Oh, I've taken you *completely* by surprise. I do love shocking people."

He sat in the rocker opposite her again and fussed with his pipe, turning the cleaning tool, tamping in tobacco. Always watching her.

"Of course, I'll make it exquisitely pleasurable for you, my dear. I am considered an extraordinary lover. People never seem to quite recover from me, I spoil them for other sex. But there's no particular rush. We can play it as a long, slow game." He began to fill the room with the fragrance of Erlich's tobacco. "I love games. That's what life is, of course. That's what I discovered at school. Rigid games with rigid rules. I decided to design my own set of games. I carry my bag of mirrors with me. I lure people into the labyrinth and down. It's very pleasurable, though the sensation of pleasure is so *distressingly* fleeting. Like the flight of a sparrow through a house, in one window and out the other. I keep hoping for higher-caliber quarry who'll prolong the delectation." She had the distinct sense that he was offering this as a challenge. "Because the moral of the game is that people fall down the dungeon stairs of their own . . . well, *sinfulness* seems a deliciously appropriate word, doesn't it?"

He looked at her without blinking, and she willed herself to meet his gaze. Her eyes prickled, and one of his looked at some vague point beyond her, but she never saw him blink. There was a small smile (seraphic or satanic?) on his face. If he were to take off his shoes, she thought, would I see cloven feet?

"I do hope you won't disappoint me, Marni," he said softly. "I've been savoring this for a long time. There's a very sentimental side to me, you know. I've had the photographs of you in my bedroom dresser for years. Ainsley found them and was wildly jealous. It was most amusing."

Marni felt curiously drugged, as though this were happening in a dream. As though totally surreal and improbable events would unfold themselves, and she would have no control and no responsibility either.

That's the seduction, she thought. (The *sinfulness*?) That's the trap: the pretense of no responsibility. The *desire* for no responsibility.

Her nerve ends stood on tiptoe, watching for secret passages away from the dungeon.

"To get down to serious matters," Geraint said. "Rule one of my own private game is that I can never have too much money to support a lifestyle in which I am constantly striving to exceed my own fantasies. So there has never been any shadow of doubt in my mind that I would inherit the Thorpe fortunes, lock, stock, and barrel."

There would just be these two tiny chinks to work with: his vanity; and his love of the chase, his desire for limited opposition.

"You could have saved yourself a lot of messiness, Geraint," she said dryly. "I had a legal renunciation drawn up before I had dinner with

Andy. I intend to show it to Abigail. Be rich and be damned for all I care."

Geraint beamed. She was being appraised as high-caliber quarry. She was doing well.

"But you see, my dear, it doesn't help at all. The Dragon Lady would almost certainly be as embarrassingly sentimental as her son. Oh, she'd breathe a little fire and smoke, of course, but she'd be itching to send him to Groton and Harvard. You couldn't stop her. A renunciation would just whet her desire, it would do the trick entirely. It would be an insulting bid for independence on your part, and she'd never allow it. You'd have Thorpe money down on you like an avalanche. And I really can't allow all that lovely fortune to be diverted away from my needy self, do you see?

"But this doesn't mean you have to suffer deprivation. Not at all. Now, here's the game plan.

"First, we'll put that Botticellian infant on the sofa where he can sleep in peace. Then we'll retire to the bedroom for several hours of delectable sport. After that, I'm afraid the two of you will have to leave the country for quite some time, because I find myself sentimentally incapable of disposing of your son. It's an esthetic weakness."

He crossed the room again and looked down at the two of them. "Yes," he sighed. "Well, it makes the game interesting. You see, when Abigail passes from among us, her estate will go to Anderson's estate. Which, as we know, will go largely to me (though of course you do not go without mention in the will). And once Abigail's gone, I'll be happy for your legal renunciation to become public.

"You may spend your exile in England or on the continent, as you wish. I'm afraid Canada is rather too uncomfortably close. But I can assure you, I'll visit you frequently, I'll keep you in comfort. You'll have absolutely the finest in care, especially during your pregnancy and at the birth of my son. And we'll have cozy little weeks at Lake Como and the like, from time to time.

"Besides, I'm sure I can find a way to keep the time reasonably short, help Abigail along her way to her leave-taking." He was back in his rocker, looking at Marni and Matthew through a photographer's frame of his hands. "I'm even toying with the idea of marrying you, though I haven't reached a final decision on that.

"Well," he smiled. "What do you think?"

Step carefully. His mood could change with a snap of the fingers. High-caliber quarry. The chase. He loves the chase.

She met his gaze. "And if I don't choose to play the game, Gerry?"

"Ah well. Then I'm afraid you'll be found guilty of the murder of your ex-husband. On the other hand, if you cooperate, the taxi driver who drove you home will turn up, establishing an hour of leaving Andy's house well before his death. And several dishes bearing Williams's fingerprints will turn up in a kitchen cupboard."

"I see." Fear sharpened every sense to razor alertness.

The chase. Vanity. Flatter his vanity.

"You know, Geraint, that I would never be able to give you full sexual attention with my child in another room. I'd never be able to enjoy myself. It would be such a waste."

"Not at all, my dear. I love to have my women fearful and distracted. Making love to the hostess of a dinner party in her kitchen while the guests are in the dining room. That sort of thing. Gives a delicious edge to activities."

Stay calm. Stay calm. Surely Jake is on the way. Keep stalling.

"Do you have your camera here, Geraint?"

"I do indeed."

"Why don't you take a mother-and-sleeping-child series before we, ah, begin the festivities?"

His eyes lit up. "Yes," he said thoughtfully, making a frame with his hands. "Yes. An excellent idea."

It was a genuine obsession. He was shooting a second roll of film when she heard the muffled hum of a car engine between snowbanks. Geraint heard it too, of course, and smiled. "You didn't disappoint me, Marni. It won't make any difference, you know. The suspense will improve with keeping." He took her chin in his hands. "I'll be there in dream after dream." Then another look altogether came into his eyes. "But there *is* a deadline. You have a week to leave the country."

Jake was in the doorway with a gun. A second car roared up to the porch.

"How embarrassingly crude," Geraint said, brushing away Jake's gun as though it were a mosquito. "You know, of course, that I'll be out on bail within hours. You don't have a thing on me."

He intercepted the look between Jake and Marni, and his eyes glittered. He bowed and blew Marni a kiss. His smile was radiant.

20: Snakes and Ladders

The note was delivered by hand to Marni's apartment on Mt. Vernon Street that evening. She knew Jake's man was watching the building, otherwise she might not have gone down to the street door when the buzzer rang. A taxi driver handed her the envelope. It was of thick cream stock, embossed with the Thorpe crest.

She carried it up in the little ancient elevator without opening it. She thought: Now a die will be cast.

Technically she had six days of Geraint's ultimatum left. But Jake had raised his eyebrows and said: "That's the thing about people like that. They underestimate everyone else."

All right, he had said. Suppose your taxi driver never comes forward; suppose no evidence of Williams's presence can be produced; suppose Ainsley cannot be pressured into testimony. There was still the forensic evidence. A lot could be learned from sedatives and poison. It was quite possible they could pinpoint a place of purchase. And even if they couldn't, a jury would have to show that Marni had purchased such commodities. There was no way she could be found guilty of murder. It was an empty threat, Jake said.

Marni knew that Geraint did not make empty threats.

She also knew, even before she left the farm, that she would defy him. She knew, therefore, that there would be repercussions.

I like to make the punishment fit the crime.

"As long as he's free," she'd said, "Matthew's life and mine will be in danger."

"We'll get him," Jake had promised. "We'll nail him."

The old elevator creaked its way to the fourth floor. Marni locked all

three bolts on her apartment door, checked the fire-escape window
and noted Jake's second man below in Acorn Street, keeping watch on
the fire escape. She kissed Matthew good night in the roll-away bed set
up in one corner of her study.

Then she opened Abigail's letter.

It was handwritten with a fountain pen containing a rich brown ink
that glowed against the cream stock. The handwriting was bold, with
flourishes. The note said simply:

*I will expect you for morning tea at ten-thirty promptly, tomorrow
morning. Yours sincerely, Abigail Thorpe.*

It did not seem to be the kind of invitation that is easily refused. I'll
go, she thought. And I'll take the legal renunciation with me. But I
won't say anything about Matthew until she does.

At ten-thirty (though not precisely, since Marni was not the sort of
person who likes to jump when a whistle is blown); at ten-thirty more
or less, having secured a baby-sitter through a bonded and
triple-checked agency, Marni stood outside the grand old Thorpe
mansion on Marlborough Street in the Back Bay. She pounded with
the huge brass knocker, and a doorman answered. He took her coat in
the hallway, and waited while she removed her boots. Then he
beckoned her to follow him. At the French doors into the huge front
room, he announced: "The young lady has arrived, ma'am."

"Yes, yes," a voice said. The voice was full of money and
age, of culture, of vibrancy, of sinewy waspishness. "Show her
in, Simpson."

Abigail sat in an armchair at the front of the room, in the arc of the
great bay window. A Miro hung in a niche on one wall. There was a
Chagall on another, and a great ornate seventeenth-century French
mirror, gilt, over the elaborately carved mantel. Abigail, who was tiny,
tapped her silver-tipped walking cane peremptorily on the polished
wood floor by way of summons.

Marni felt, simultaneously, anger and amusement. Abigail took as a
given that the world was at her beck and call. When she was eighteen,

a green bride, a Ukrainian kid from Jamica Plain, Marni had been terrified of her. Now she thought: What a magnificent old ruin.

Abigail was so tiny that her feet did not quite reach the floor. The delicate white halo of hair flared out like angel dust against the maroon wing chair. An inner dynamo of energy flinched and sang along the nerve paths of her eighty years. Marni thought of humming birds. She walked across the room to her former mother-in-law.

"Pour the tea for me," Abigail said.

There was a mahogany trolley beside her, laden with heavy silver and Royal Albert china. There was a silver strainer, and there were lemon quarters in a little silver dish.

"It's Earl Grey," Abigail said. "I seem to recall you like it."

"Thank you. Yes, I do," Marni said. She poured Abigail a cup and offered sugar and lemon. She poured a cup for herself.

"Sit down," Abigail said, indicating the other wing chair across the bay.

Abigail stirred her tea for a long time, then she sipped it in silence. Sometimes she stared out the windows into the bare branches of the magnolia tree on snowy Marlborough Street. Sometimes she looked meditatively at Marni. Sometimes she looked at her jubilant Chagall as though it might give her inspiration.

"Well," she said at last, and there was something in her voice that Marni had never heard before. A tremor. "You had dinner with him. How was he?"

Marni swallowed. She saw again Andy's gaunt face and frail form in the candlelight across the dining table. Her first love, her mentor, the father of her son, her dear friend. The numbness, the shock that had settled on her ever since Joseph Lucyk's death and had somehow propelled her through these nightmarish days, now cracked. She put her hands over her face. It was several seconds before she could speak. "He was . . . contented," she said. "He was planning to go to Europe."

She glanced up. Abigail was looking at her very intently. Abigail's eyes were very bright. Shimmering. If Marni hadn't listened to an encyclopedia of stories about the Dragon Lady, she would have said Abigail's eyes were bright with unshed tears.

"I heard he had AIDS," Abigail said quietly, watching.

Marni blinked.

"Was he suffering?" Abigail asked, looking away.

"A little, I think," Marni said. Anything other than the truth would have seemed tacky in that room, against the sterling silver and the bright bright eyes. "He was very weak. But not . . . unhappy."

Abigail held her walking stick with both hands and traced a scroll in a Bokhara rug with the silver tip. "Did he mention me?"

"Yes. He was going to Europe so you wouldn't know. He didn't want to hurt you."

Abigail suddenly heaved herself out of her chair and moved restlessly around the room, the thud of the walking stick punctuating her movements. "It's a terrible thing," she said, "to let pride. . . ." She made a circuit of the room, leaving the sentence unfinished. "It's a terrible thing for a child to die before a parent. An unnatural thing."

Her circuit brought her in front of Marni. "I always knew, you know. About his. . . . I realized when he was thirteen or fourteen. No, earlier. When he first brought the Finnbar boy here for the Christmas vacation. I thought it would hurt him less if I pretended never to know. So I spent a lifetime playing at wringing my hands at his playboy game."

She sighed heavily and slumped back in her armchair. "Could you pour me another cup, my dear?" she asked almost plaintively. "I adored him," she said. "Maybe it harmed him, I don't know." Marni handed her the cup. "I was furious with you," she said, "for not playing along. Keeping up appearances."

She sipped her tea in silence for so long that Marni wondered if the "interview" was over. Suddenly Abigail said: "I liked you."

Marni, caught off guard, said without thinking: "I was frightened of you. But I always had a sneaking admiration for you too."

"You don't like me?"

"I think, if I hadn't been afraid of you, I would have. I think I do now."

"Good," Abigail said, as though a treaty had been signed. She punctuated the agreement with a thump of her cane.

She leaned forward, very serious. "Was it the Finnbar boy who killed him?"

Marni was so startled that she spilled a quantity of Earl Grey into her saucer.

"Well, it certainly wasn't you," Abigail said.

"Have you read the tabloids?" Marni asked.

"No," Abigail said sharply. "Simpson brought them in, but I don't read trash. It was the Finnbar boy, wasn't it?"

"Yes," Marni said. "But there'll never be proof, I'm afraid. And he is quite certain that I'll be found guilty."

Abigail became rather agitated, heaving herself out of her chair, again, thudding her way around the room, talking jerkily. "Right from the start, I knew it would be disastrous. Right from that first Christmas. The boys were ten years old, I think. The Finnbar boy used to pocket silver: spoons, saltshakers, candlesticks, things like that. He could lie to your face, smooth as cream. Well, we'll deal with that, of course. We'll deal with that. Yes." She kept walking, sometimes holding onto a chair for balance and waving her cane, talking to herself. "Yes, we'll deal with that. Yes, indeed."

It was as though she had been tightly wound and would walk till the spring uncoiled. First the talking petered out, then the brandishing of the cane, then the walking. She slumped into her chair.

"Now," she said briskly. "The child. My grandson. I want to see him."

Marni gasped and shook her head with disbelief. "How long have you known?"

"Only this week, in fact. The hospital. The daughter of friends on the Symphony Board is a nurse. But I always thought perhaps. . . . I always hoped, as a matter of fact."

Marni sighed. "And all these years I was so afraid. . . . All these wasted years. I have something for you." She took the legal-renunciation document from her purse and gave it to Abigail.

"What's this?" Abigail said testily. "I can't read without my glasses. What is it?"

"It's a legal document renouncing any inheritance rights for Matthew."

"Don't insult me," Abigail said, ripping it in two. "And don't make me angry. I need all my energy to fight Anderson's will in probate. You think I'll tolerate that Finnbar boy touching any of it?"

She clattered her cup against her saucer and fumed a little. When she calmed down she said again: "My grandson. I'd like to see him this afternoon. The wake's tomorrow and we'll have to buy him clothes, I imagine."

"Mrs. Thorpe," Marni said, annoyed. It was her turn to pace. "I do like you. I am happy . . . I *think* I'm happy that you want to claim your grandson. But I will not let you run his life or mine. I will *not.*"

For a moment, it seemed as though fire might leap from Abigail's nostrils. Then she laughed. "All right," she said. "All right."

She poured herself more tea and was suddenly enormously animated. "Can you keep a secret?" she asked.

"I expect so."

"You must swear to keep this one. Swear on the head of my cane."

Was she serious? Marni's eyebrows went up as Abigail extended toward her the carved and scrolled silver head of her walking stick.

"Swear," she ordered. "Place your hand on the cane and swear."

"I swear," Marni said.

"All right, then. We will get the Finnbar boy the only way such boys can be got. We trip them up on their own wickedness." She dropped her voice to a whisper, her eyes glittering. "This is something I learned from the Borgias. I love history, you know, especially Renaissance history. People had such *energy* then. Now, I must show you something." She called for Simpson and asked him to bring her jewel box. She extracted a man's ring, a double circlet of gold, carved, scrolled with the Thorpe crest, surmounted by a large ruby.

"This was my husband's," she said. "And Anderson always loved it. But I wouldn't let him have it until after my death, mainly because I knew the Finnbar boy would weasel it away from him. He could never say no to that wretched boy. Three times the Finnbar boy stole this ring, three times I caught him. Found it among his things. Three times, of course, he denied knowing anything about it with the most innocent amazement. Well," she said. "Well."

But then she fell silent for so long that Marni had to prompt her. "Yes?" she murmured, touching Abigail's wrist.

Abigail, as though nudged from sleep, started. "Of course," she said, as though picking up where she had left off, "the Finnbar boy will come to the wake and the funeral. Without a shadow of a doubt. He'll be very public and charming, you know how he is. And so will we be. But I'll let the word get around that the Thorpe ring is in the pocket of Anderson's jacket, because he always loved it so. Of course, the Finnbar boy won't be able to resist it. He'll steal it again. He won't be able to resist putting it on, flaunting it here and there. And that will be that, you see?"

Marni did not quite see, but her nerves were taut with the prospect of having to face Geraint at the funeral. Of course, Abigail was right. Geraint would be there, publicly grieving, privately flaunting power. I need to tell Jake, she thought. I'll feel safer if he's there.

"Now," Abigail said briskly, "when you bring my grandson, we can discuss schools. I think the family tradition should be maintained."

"Mrs. Thorpe!" Something stubborn in Marni wrenched itself away from preoccupation with Geraint and marshaled itself against another form of attack on Matthew. "Oscar Wilde said that you can't call a man truly depraved unless he's been to a very expensive boarding school. I firmly intend that Matthew will go to a good public school."

"What!" Abigail said, banging her stick on the floor.

"Especially since Geraint Finnbar went to the same school as Anderson."

"Well, we'll see. We'll see," grumbled Abigail. "I admit you have a point. And what about you, child? What about this real-estate business?"

"Oh, it's hard to think about anything except. . . ." Marni gestured wearily. "I suppose I have to go on making a living. I'd still love to salvage houses in the inner city. Turn neighborhoods around. But I've been fired from my company. And it's impossible to get financial backing for high-risk areas."

"Hmm," Abigail said. And the glitter was back in her eyes. "I'd rather like to turn neighborhoods around, too. I might consider that sort of business partnership." She tapped the floor meditatively with her cane. "Yes, I might indeed," she said.

At the wake and at the funeral, Geraint Finnbar, who came with a beautiful young woman on his arm, was the essence of solicitous grief. He moved among the guests, dispensing his sorrowful charm, conferring blessings with his mellow voice. He took Mrs. Thorpe's arm and helped her down the steps from the church. At the Marlborough Street "At Home" that followed the funeral, he brought her sherry. He moved among the guests. He touched Marni's arm several times in passing, and once he touched her cheek.

Sergeant Jake Murphy, another guest, sipped sherry but could have done with a beer. His eyes rarely left Geraint Finnbar. "I like them when they get this blasé," he told Marni. "It's always their own hubris that does them in."

"I wish I could be so confident," Marni said anxiously. Heart in mouth, she watched as Geraint stooped to chat with Matthew. She heard him promise to take the boy sailing and riding in the spring.

Matthew was enchanted with Uncle Gerry.

Just before leaving, Geraint murmured in Marni's ear: "My dear, you do make the game delightfully interesting. But three days have gone by, and I detect no preparations whatsoever for leaving the country. I'm afraid you have broken the rules quite flagrantly. I'm afraid there will have to be reprisals." He smiled, bowed slightly, and left.

"What did he say?" Jake demanded.

"He said there will have to be reprisals."

"There will indeed," Jake said. Through the window he could see the car that would tail Geraint edge from the curb.

Marni looked across the room at Abigail.

Abigail smiled. She made her way slowly through the last guests, tapping her stick. She drew Marni aside. "The ring was gone," she said. "I went to the funeral parlor before the church service, for the closing of the casket. I gave my son my last blessing." She pressed a handkerchief to her lips and eyes and said nothing for several seconds. "I checked his pocket," she said gruffly. "The ring had gone. So that is that, my dear."

"Geraint said there will be repercussions. I'm frightened."

"Repercussions," Abigail said. "Yes."

"We haven't heard the last of him," Marni said.

"Oh, I believe we have, my dear. The ring, the ring."

"I don't know what you mean."

Abigail raised her eyebrows. "Didn't I explain? Perhaps not. Not fully. Well, you see, yesterday, I doctored the ring a little. I filed the inside, roughened it . . . if you'd had a magnifying glass, you would have seen a sharp point on the inside curve. I coated it with a little something the Borgias recommended. It enters the blood, works slowly, takes three or four days to act. The wearer falls asleep one night, and doesn't wake up again."

Marni felt visceral relief and shock in equal parts. Her hand flew to her mouth.

Abigail raised her eyebrows. "Well, I don't see how a shadow of moral blame could fall on me, do you? As far as I'm concerned, the ring was to be buried with my son. If a thief wanted to interfere. . . ." She shrugged. "Then I think it would be an absolutely appropriate, absolutely fitting conclusion, don't you? A very proper death, indeed."

21: Sun-Dried Tomatoes, Kids, Love, the Meaning Of Life and All That

Jake and his three children stood waiting on Mt. Vernon Street for Marni to push the buzzer that would release the locks on the outer door. It was mid-March, and the snow had turned to slush, and Kathy thought she saw a crocus beside the statue of Christopher Columbus in Louisberg Square. All four were nervous.

"You have to behave," Jake warned them. "It's not the kind of apartment you can just run wild in. You have to—"

"Uncle Joe lets us do whatever we want at his place," Brian offered belligerently. Uncle Joe was a widower, "just a friend, that's all, a *kind* man," who took Judy, Jake's former wife, out to dinner once a week.

"Well, that's nice," Jake said. "It's nice that Uncle Joe—"

"Is she snotty?" ten-year-old Kathy asked.

"No," he said emphatically. "No, she's not snotty at all. She's very nice. But she's—well, she just likes things to look very nice. I don't want you messing up her apartment." He pushed the button beside her apartment number again.

"Are you in love with her?" demanded Brian, just as Marni caught them off guard by opening the door herself.

Jake blushed crimson. "Uh, *kids*," he offered awkwardly, spreading his hands in a gesture of helplessness. "They have a knack for the embarrassing. . . ." He laughed nervously.

Marni smiled. "Matthew's upstairs. Come on up."

In her living room, the children circled each other warily, like puppies in a playground.

Brian went to the fridge and took out a Coke. "Mom says the

195

fancier the kitchen, the lousier the cook," he said. But then, minutes later: "Hey! That's neat. The way your fire escape goes right by the window. Can I go out on it, Dad?" He didn't wait for an answer. He opened the window and swung his legs across the sill.

"I want to, I want to," Jake Junior cried, jumping up and down.

"I want to, I want to," Matthew echoed.

"Well, you can't," Brian said, from the fire escape. "You're too little." He slammed the window down from outside.

"I got cars," Matthew said, standing on one foot, locking the other around his ankle. "In a box in my room."

"Okay," Jake Junior said.

There was a roar of *vroom vrooms* from the study, the Indy 500 tearing across eiderdown, up sheets, and down pillows on the roll-away bed.

"You got any magazines?" Kathy asked. She found a pile beside the TV and sprawled on the living-room carpet, leafing through them.

Jake and Marni, a little tense, embarrassed, faced each other in the tiny kitchen.

"Well," she said.

"Well," he said. "How's Eva?"

"She's doing fine. She can go home in a couple of weeks. Steve's parents are going to stay at the farm for a while to look after the children."

"And Abigail?"

"Oh Abigail." She threw up her hands. "Has half of City Council and Jamaica Plain cowering in fear. Not to mention every bank manager between here and Concord. She's going to overhaul the whole inner city, I think."

"Aren't you going to ask the G question?" Jake demanded.

It was a sort of game now that all the charges against Marni had been dropped. It had become a tradition already. She and Abigail played it, too—with a different twist. She could not tell Jake about the ring. It was a secret between Abigail and herself. A weighty secret.

"Okay," she said. "Any sign of Geraint or his body?"

"No sign. He saw the net had closed in. I don't know how he

managed it . . . well, influence, of course . . . but he's out of the country. Europe, South America, we may never know where he disappeared to. It's Interpol's problem now."

"I'll still sleep easier when I hear—"

"He'll never get back in, that's certain." Jake put his arms around her. "Your one week deadline's well behind us, and nothing's happened. His pride would never allow that, would it?"

"You're right." Yes, she thought, that was the most potent evidence. Somewhere there was a corpse with a ring on its finger. *Accessory after the fact*, a voice whispered inside her head. *Justifiable self-defence*, another voice whispered back. You exchange one moral conundrum for another one, she thought uneasily. But Matthew was safe, an unambiguous good. "Well, I'll stop worrying then."

"Good," he said. "Oh, almost forgot. I brought you something." He'd wrapped it, she noted, not too expertly, in dove-gray paper flecked with white butterflies. Both the thought and the slight clumsiness evoked such a sudden tenderness in her that she felt dizzy.

"Let me guess," she said. "Um. Perfume?"

"No." He was dreadfully embarrassed now. He couldn't bear to have the guessing game continue. The gift had seemed the height of appropriateness and sophistication when he bought it. "It's sun-dried tomatoes," he said.

"Oh, Jake, how lovely, how very . . ." She began laughing helplessly, partly out of nervousness, partly out of delight. He began laughing too. Their laughter bounced and ricocheted and escalated and the children all hung in the door, wide-eyed, and began to laugh too. It was a symphony, a rock concert of laughter. The children shrieked and rolled on the floor. They all laughed till the tears ran down their cheeks.

"I love you," he said.

She bit her lip and smiled and began laughing again. "Let's walk down to the Common," she said. "And see if the ducklings are there yet."

Hooray, hooray, cheered the children.

Somewhere in the middle of the hubbub of getting coats on, under the chatter of the children, she said to him: "I love you too, Jake."

They kissed under cover of the open fridge door, watched only by the sun-dried tomatoes.

Come on, come on, the children called, and they were all in the hallway, waiting for the tiny and elderly elevator. It blundered up to their floor and opened just as Marni heard the phone ring in the closed apartment.

"It might be Eva," she said. "You go on down. I'll answer it and join you in a minute."

It was still ringing when she had fumbled with the keys for all three locks and got back through the door.

"Hello?" she said.

A very cultured voice answered, a voice she had not heard for weeks, a voice with a very faint British cast to it (as though the accent were not quite focused) and with a mocking hesitancy on the *s* sounds. "Could I speak to Matthew, please?"